SHAMROCKS AND SURPRISES

A HOLIDAY BEACH SWEET ROMANCE

ELLE RUSH

"Lucky" Lucy Callahan can fix anything, which is why her boss sent her to the Dew Drop Inn in Holiday Beach, Minnesota. The neglected hotel sounds like the perfect challenge for a woman who likes to bring things to their full potential.

Roy Wagner would happily see the Dew Drop Inn go up in a blaze of glory after the trouble it has caused his family. He'd even supply the marshmallows. He doesn't know what Lucy is doing in town, but he's certain the relentlessly helpful, happy woman is up to no good.

Rebuilding a hotel is no easy task, especially when her new neighbor insists that she won't be able to make the old hotel fit into Holiday Beach's unique tourist-friendly setting, but Lucy hasn't failed yet. If she can get Roy on her side, maybe she can convince him that the changes she's bringing could be a very good thing for him and his hometown.

Join Elle Rush's newsletter to keep up with her latest releases and other news at www.ellerush.com/newsletter.

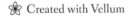

CHAPTER 1

"YOU HAVE GOT to be kidding me." Lucy Callahan slammed on the brakes and looked at the building in front of her in disbelief. After leaving Minneapolis and driving north for three hours, the GPS in her rental car was informing her she had arrived at her destination. "*This* is D.D.I. Limited?" She grabbed her phone off the passenger seat and opened the recording app. "February sixteenth. Note to self. Is it legal in Minnesota to kill your boss for gross misrepresentation? Because I'm not sure if even I can fix this wreck."

She shifted her rented SUV into park and gave the building a second, scrutinizing look. Plywood covered a circular window in an attic gable, at least four windows were missing shutters, and one of the eaves hung from the corner of the roof, laden with icicles. And that was just on the front of the building. "Check out this property for me, he said. It'll be an easy project for you, he said," Lucy muttered to herself. "You won't need much budget, he said." A gust of wind rocked the already leaning Dew Drop Inn sign. "I'm getting my budget tripled. At least."

The small hotel sat on the north side of Spruce Line Drive, at the edge of Holiday Beach, Minnesota. After studying the property maps and records, Lucy knew a corner of the property ran into Star Lake, at the edge of the town's public beach. The inn itself was fifty years old and, was still mostly original. It had two stories, sixteen standard rooms, four suites, two conference rooms that could be combined into one big one, an exercise room, an outdoor pool, and a large parking lot which it shared with the business next door.

The bar looked to be in much better shape than its neighbor, despite the six inches of snow on the palm-thatched portico outside the front door. Patio lanterns hung inside the windows, making blobs of color visible across the parking lot. The neon beer signs beneath them, and the Hawaiian shirt clad people walking past in the background, finished setting the mood, and its warm cheerfulness called to her. It was exactly what Lucy needed after a full day of travel which culminated in a discouraging ending.

A blast of warm air and the scent of coconut hit her as she walked through the door. More patio lights hung over the bar, and flags from various Polynesian and Caribbean countries hung on the walls amid pictures of palm trees and hammocks on beaches. Two young people, a man and a woman in their early twenties wearing Hawaiian shirts, worked the room, and a tall, beefy man who looked like a lumberjack dressed as Jimmy Buffett stood behind the bar. "Welcome to the

Escape Room," he called to her as Lucy stood, stunned, in the doorway. "What can I get you? It's margarita night."

Lucy stared at the five blenders on the counter behind him. "What a coincidence, that's exactly what I didn't know I wanted. A lime margarita on the rocks, please," she ordered. Then she laughed, because she was still fully encased in her ski jacket, gloves, and scarf in a tropical paradise. She slipped off her coat and stuffed her knit winter set down the sleeve and hopped on a well-worn wooden stool. "This is a welcome surprise. I didn't expect to find a tiki bar this far north."

In fact, when she'd done her research of Holiday Beach, she wasn't sure it was big enough to have a bar at all. The town's website was sorely out of date. The sole picture they had of Main Street didn't show any of the shops or restaurants she'd seen as she'd driven through town. The fact that the town could support so many businesses, coupled with all the houses she'd seen, also doubled the population the website listed. Until she'd arrived, Lucy had been concerned the area had no need for a hotel. Now that she'd seen the hotel itself, she was worried there was enough business for two or three, and the Dew Drop Inn would come in last.

"We don't get a lot of visitors in Holiday Beach this time of year," the bartender said.

"I imagine most people head south at the beginning of January for a sunny getaway and don't come back till March but I'm here for work," Lucy said.

"Then you'll get to experience Holiday Beach in all

its February in Minnesota glory. We've got snow, we've got ice, we've got frost. Aren't you lucky?" he asked with teasing, fake enthusiasm.

Lucy's planned tropical vacation the previous winter had been cancelled due to do circumstances beyond her control, leaving her available for a job in northern Wyoming. Then she'd spent the summer in Alaska, before two glorious months working in California in the fall. Now she was back with a starring role in *Frozen* 3. "I'm really not. I'm Lucy," she added, smiling at her own joke. If she was going to be in town for a while, it wouldn't hurt to introduce herself to a few people. Getting to know the resident bartender was always a good way for introductions to other locals.

"I'm Roy Wagner. Welcome to my establishment."

It made sense that he was the owner. Unlike the other two younger employees, Roy was in his late thirties or early forties; it was hard to tell in the neon glow, although the lines around his eyes made Lucy guess older. His large build and deep tan, even in winter, proclaimed that he spent his free time outside, perhaps juggling logs or bench-pressing cabins. But he wasn't a scary-looking huge. He had a friendly, open smile, and a good sense of humor, from what she could tell from their brief interaction.

"Thank you. Expect to see me often. I'm expecting this project to be pretty challenging."

"I'll look forward to it. We have Margarita Night on Mondays, and Drafty Thursdays, which is also darts night. We also have a live band every other weekend, which makes it easy to dance your cares away." He slipped an umbrella-topped glass in front of her, then excused himself to talk to some new customers.

When he returned to check on her, he asked if she needed some food with her beverage. "We don't have a kitchen, but we have some snacks, so you aren't drinking and driving on an empty stomach," he said.

"According to my GPS, I have arrived at my destination. Thanks, though."

Roy's smile disappeared. "Are you staying next door?"

"At the Dew Drop Inn? Yes."

"There's a Fairlane Motel about three miles up the road that I can recommend."

It wasn't a good sign when locals tried to send people to the competition. Even worse, this was a friendly suggestion. As a bar owner, the hotel was no threat to Roy's business. In fact, with the shared parking lot, he should want more people to stay there since it likely meant more business for him. Now she actively dreaded walking into the Dew Drop Inn and discovering what awaited her. Lucy had been demoralized when she'd seen how much work there was to do on the exterior. The interior must be nightmare-inducing. "I saw the outside of the Dew Drop looked like it needed a little work," Lucy said.

"The whole place is a dump," Roy said bluntly. "I'd ask your boss if you can be relocated for the duration."

"That won't happen," Lucy said. "But I appreciate the warning."

"Good luck, then. I'm sure we'll be seeing a lot of you."

"I hope so. I like the feel of your bar." She rarely found an establishment with such good vibes on her first day in a new place. This time it was a bar. Usually she had to ask around to find a diner or a coffee shop she could turn into her home away from home while she was on a project. This time, she'd found it on her own, right next door.

A smile burst across her face when Roy waved at her as she walked out the door. Maybe her luck was finally changing.

CHAPTER 2

THE FRONT STEPS were cleared of snow, which was a good start. Lucy hauled her overnight bag and a suitcase to the check-in desk. She'd make a second trip to the car for the rest once she had her room.

The reception area was spotless, another good sign. The door frames, trim, and welcome desk were all solid wood. The rest of the décor was stuck firmly in the seventies. Lucy could hear it begging for an upgrade, which was fine with her. After a decade of property maintenance, she knew where to invest to get the biggest bang for a buck, and the lobby was a big one. But she had a lot of other areas still to inspect.

She heard rustling through the open office door behind the counter. "Hello?" she called.

"Be right with you." Seconds later, a pretty brunette woman stepped out. Lucy judged her to be in her midtwenties, barely, with a flustered look and a determined smile on her face. "Welcome to the Dew Drop Inn. How can I help you?"

The hand-written sign on the counter said the assistant manager on duty was Gloria Vargas. Lucy was expecting a man named Roger Lucius, with whom she'd been arranging her stay and duties. "Is Mr. Lucius in?"

"I'm sorry, Mr. Lucius left the company at the end of January. I'm sure I can be of assistance. Did you have a reservation?"

That was news to her. But it also explained a lot, like why she'd been warned the Dew Drop Inn would not be her standard assignment. She had a file full of repair requests that went back five years, and they were all signed by different people. If the hotel couldn't hold on to a manager, it wasn't surprising that nothing got done. "Yes, for a suite. My name is Lucy Callahan." Gloria's pleasant but blank nod meant her name didn't ring any bells. "There won't be any billing information because it's being comped by the company. I'm a property maintenance manager for Longfellow Family Hotels. I'm here to assess the inn for the head office and manage any required repairs or renovations," she added.

"Oh." Gloria looked up from the computer screen. "Was I supposed to know you were coming? Am I supposed to have anything special organized for you?"

It was late, she'd been travelling all day, and she had another suitcase and groceries still in the car. "Yes, but I'm not starting work today, so we don't have to worry about it right now. If you give me my room and the wi-fi code, I'll email the head office, and ask them to contact you. We can meet in the morning, or I can speak to the day manager." Going over all her instructions again with a new person, and then waiting for them to organize what she needed was a pain, but it wasn't the first time Lucy's arrival was a surprise to staff.

"I am the day manager. I'm also the night manager until Mr. Lucius's replacement arrives. In the meantime, I'll be happy to help you in the morning." Gloria slipped a key card over the counter. "I put you in the Emerald Suite. It's on the main floor. Please let me know if I can help with anything else or if you have any problems."

"That sounds great. I'll bring in the rest of my luggage and see you tomorrow."

Lucy had barely set down her suitcase to open the door to her suite when she heard a noise. A tall, blonde woman pushing a housekeeping cart exited the room at the end of the hall. The wheels squeaked loudly, and the other woman sighed before she saw Lucy. "Good afternoon," she said. "Can I help you with something in your room?"

"I'm just checking in, thanks." If anyone knew problem areas in the hotel, it would be the woman who'd have to clean them. "I'm Lucy Callahan. I'm a property maintenance manager from Longfellow Family Hotels' head office. I'll be working here for the next few weeks."

"Brooke Portman. It's nice to meet you. What does a property maintenance manager do?"

That answered another one of Lucy's questions as to how long it had been since anyone had looked over the Dew Drop Inn. "I ensure necessary repairs and general maintenance are being done on the property. I also determine if any upgrades or changes should be made." The blonde's eyes got bigger as Lucy continued her explanation. "I'll be looking around the hotel for the next couple weeks, but I'd like to set up a time to ask you a few questions about problem areas I might not find on my own."

Brooke nodded hard, and Lucy knew the woman already had a list in mind. "My daughter is at volleyball practice every night this week, but if we can do it in the afternoon, that works for me. It's nice to meet you, Ms. Callahan. Be sure to let me know if you need anything special while you're here."

"I will, thanks." The fact the staff was friendly, although unprepared, gave Lucy hope.

Brooke and her squeaky cart continued down the hall and around the corner, and Lucy returned to her suitcase. The door opened easily, and she stepped into her suite.

It was old enough to be retro and updated enough for the new pieces to be jarring. She knew she could fix the building, but if the rest of the rooms were like this, the Dew Drop Inn needed an interior designer too. Lucy noted with satisfaction that the bedspread lay evenly on the mattress, showing off the fact it didn't have any telltale dips to give away its age. The towels were fresh and thick, and there were two extra blankets in the cupboard.

The problem was the motley assortment of furniture. No amount of wax and polish could erase the scars and gouges in the wooden headboard or the desk beside the window. The mirror over the newer, press-board dresser was old enough to be an antique, but that also meant it had weird spotting on the back of the glass which left black areas that offered no reflection.

"It'll be two weeks, three weeks tops, he said," Lucy muttered to her reflection. "I'm not going to be out of here before spring." That was if she was lucky, and she knew better than to count on luck. Fortunately, she always packed for a worst-case scenario. The Dew Drop Inn qualified. After she brought her second load of luggage in from her car, she finished exploring her suite.

The kitchenette was compact but had everything she needed. The small bar fridge, toaster oven, coffee pot, and microwave would do for the next month, or however long it took for her to do her job.

Lucy dropped onto the bed and sighed in delight at the firm mattress. She stretched out for the first time since she'd left Boston that morning. Two flights and a three-hour drive made for a long day. She'd stopped at a grocery store on her way through Holiday Beach and had enough for supper that night and breakfast the next morning. By then, she'd know what she'd need to get through the rest of the week.

As she stared at the crack-free ceiling—one thing she didn't have to worry about—she wondered how this had become her life: flying around the country, living out of hotel rooms, eating out almost every night. She'd traversed the country multiple times and had seen and experienced enough to make a world traveler jealous.

She couldn't imagine another career that would give her the same opportunities. If not for the part of her job where she crawled around in furnace rooms and examined garbage chutes, she could be mistaken for a celebrity jetsetter.

Lucy didn't mind the lack of glamour. She was exceptionally good at what she did, and she was proud of it. Growing up the daughter of an apartment manager, she knew all the ins and outs of minor household repairs by the time she hit high school. Summer jobs with a local landscaper during college gave her experience with everything outside.

It wasn't all room service and free flights, though. She'd had the same tiny one-bedroom apartment for the last decade, since she wasn't home long enough to need anything bigger. Her last two relationships had sputtered and died like her annual windowsill geranium, and for the same reason—lack of attention. Lucy could say she was great at keeping in touch online; she maintained dozens of friendships and keep in contact with her extended family on a weekly basis, but she lacked experience when it came to in-person relationships. It wasn't easy when she was gone for weeks at a time and was only home long enough to do laundry and get a new assignment.

But she wasn't in Holiday Beach to bemoan her personal life, or lack of it. She needed to recover from her travel day so she could hit the ground running in the morning. The frozen lasagna she'd picked up at the grocery store would only take five minutes to heat. But the mattress was comfortable, and she had lots of time for supper. She'd plan things better tomorrow: eat first, then head to the bar to see what the bartender recommended on a Tuesday. Because he'd probably smile at her again when he served it up and wouldn't that be a great way to end the day. She'd get up. In a minute.

CHAPTER 3

"YOU ASKED me to remind you when it was six thirty, boss."

Roy Wagner twisted the coupler into the keg and turned the handle. "Thanks, Emily." A minute later he stood and opened the faucet to make sure the beer flowed properly. "I'll be back after the meeting to close down and cash out."

"You don't have to rush, Roy. Mickey can handle it. Besides, I think we've already had our excitement for the day."

There had been excitement? "We did? What was it?" The Escape Room saw as much action as it normally did, but that wasn't saying much, especially in the dead of winter. The summer was an entirely different situation. But five months into a Minnesota winter, money was tight, and nerves were tighter. Roy couldn't afford to miss a single opportunity if he wanted to keep making his payroll. He'd been at the bar since they'd opened at four. He was certain he'd greeted all of their dozen customers personally.

"The stranger you were talking to. I saw her carrying luggage into the Dew Drop Inn. Did she say what she's doing in Holiday Beach? Is she a movie scout?" his waitress and backup bartender asked. Emily Jardine ate, breathed, and slept acting. The twenty-two-year-old was always on the lookout for something that could whisk her out of Minnesota to Hollywood, even though she'd had two auditions and no acting jobs in the year and a half she'd worked for him.

"Lucy?"

"Was that her name?"

"Yes." Roy wasn't going to forget anything about Lucy in a hurry. A beautiful woman walking into his bar out of the blue had made his week, and that was before he'd even said hello. "She didn't say anything about being a movie scout, but if she was, I don't think she'd be staying at the Dew Drop Inn. It's hardly Hollywood quality."

He would be the one to know. Roy had grown up next to the old hotel. His parents had built the bar next door to it before he was born. Now it was his. The Escape Room had gone through many iterations over the decades: a community bar, an English pub, a sports lounge, and a forgettable couple years as a blues bar. Now it was a tiki bar, offering a tropical getaway in an arctic climate. In all that time, the Dew Drop Inn had remained the same, down to the types of flowers they put in the planters every spring. The hotel was only a couple years older than the bar, but Roy was determined to outlast it. The meeting he was about to attend was part of that plan.

"Call me if you have any problems."

"Why are you asking her? Not that Emily isn't capable, but I am the assistant manager," a new voice said, entering the conversation.

"I didn't know you were here, Mickey," Roy said. He hadn't seen his brother come through the front door and hadn't seen his coat hanging in the staff room.

Some days, the fifteen-year gap between him and his younger brother was more obvious than others, and this was one of them. Mickey stared at him with hard, brown eyes. "I've been here since my shift started. I've been cleaning, organizing and inventorying the storage room. You specifically said you wanted it done today." Mickey peeled off his coat, which was covered in a light film of dirt.

"Why you didn't check in with me when you arrived?" Now Roy had to redo the payroll to give Mickey back the thirty minutes he'd docked him for being late.

"Emily knew I was back there. I assumed you saw me too."

"Well, I didn't. And you can't work like that. You're filthy."

"Which is why I brought a towel and a fresh shirt so I could clean up before working the front of the house. This isn't my first day, Roy."

No, it wasn't. It wasn't even Mickey's first year, but he constantly acted like it was. The kid didn't have a practical bone in his body. He constantly failed to follow long-established protocols and was always suggesting wild marketing ploys. It all said he wasn't taking the assistant manager position seriously. Roy had been hesitant to give it to him the previous fall. Now he was almost positive he'd made a mistake.

"Fine. Mickey, you're in charge. Call me if you have a problem," Roy said before he headed to the office to grab his coat.

"When have we ever had to call you with a problem?" Mickey asked.

"There's always a first time."

"Mickey's got this. Go do your Chamber of Commerce stuff. Leave the bar to Mickey and the margarita making to the Queen of the Blender, boss." Emily flicked her ruby red nails at him. "Shoo!"

It didn't take long to drive from the bar to the community center. Holiday Beach was home to almost ten thousand full-time residents, not including the folks who came out to their cabins on Star Lake in the summer, but few were out after supper in the cold.

The Chamber of Commerce met at the River Street Community Center twice a month. Mostly, it was a chance for the various business owners around town to talk and come up with promotional ideas. Holiday Beach didn't have a single industry to support it, like the meat processing plant half an hour south in Bixby, so they'd had to find a way to bring business to them.

The obvious choice had been a play on their name. Since they were in cottage country, local business had run with the holidays from Easter to Hallowe'en and turned each into a multi-day event. Over the years, the town had managed to build up a reputation among summer tourists as the place to be for special occasions for the whole family. Lately they'd been trying to add winter sports and holidays so they could become a year-round destination, but it was a slow process.

Now that Christmas was over and the Valentine's sweethearts had their moment, they had to put their plans for the upcoming summer into effect.

Roy barely had time to fill his travel mug with coffee and take a seat before Josh Huntington, the Chamber of Commerce president, called the meeting to order. "Thanks for saving me a seat," he whispered to Tripp Turner, a classmate who had joined the Navy right out of high school but was now back in Holiday Beach.

"I knew you were going to be late," Tripp replied quietly. "What was it this time?"

"An empty keg and a gossip-hungry bartender."

Tripp's eyebrows went up. "What's the gossip? Habibah will want to know."

Roy laughed at the half lie. The gossip would be as much for Tripp as it would be for his wife. "It's nothing. There's a guest at the Dew Drop Inn. Emily's first guess was a Hollywood executive."

"Of course it was." His friend's attention returned to Josh, who was reviewing the last meeting's minutes. "That's not gossip. Who was the guest?"

"I don't know, but I wish her luck if she has to stay there for more than two nights."

As soon as the floor opened to new business, Roy's

hand shot in the air. "I have an update regarding the town business bylaws. By the Cup has placed a window order with Sam French and the Starlight Gallery, which means all the businesses on Main Street and Lakeside Drive are now in accordance with Holiday Beach's commercial regulations. The only holdouts left in town are Lakeside Cones and Sundaes and the Dew Drop Inn. The Dew Drop Inn has been promising for almost a year to get their signature window fixed. If they don't get it done in by the end of the month, they'll be in default for their membership in the chamber of commerce. I think we should prepare to strike them from the roll," he added with relish.

The Dew Drop Inn's management, or lack thereof, had been a thorn in the side of the council for as long as both had existed. Roy was glad that others found the business as irritating as he did. The property was a mess, chronically in disrepair, and no manager stayed longer than a year, meaning nobody had stuck around to improve the mess they'd inherited. As far as Roy was concerned, the whole town would be better off if the place shut down and decayed into dust.

"Fine, Roy. I'll go and introduce myself as the president of the Chamber of Commerce and speak to whoever's in charge. I'll tell them they're out of time," Josh said. "And, no, I'm not going to let you do it. You'll let your personal feelings get in the way. We all know how you feel about the way the Dew Drop Inn does business as your neighbor."

They didn't know the half of it, Roy thought. The bar and hotel could have had an amazing partnership;

instead, they'd been at odds since the doors opened. At this point, it was a matter of waiting to see which business closed first. Roy was determined it wouldn't be his.

The rest of the two-hour meeting was full of talk about the upcoming council-sponsored snowmobile poker derby, and the Valentine decorations which had to come down and be replaced with St. Patrick's Day ones. It was a never-ending job to keep the décor up to date, but with the town's reputation for having a different celebration every month, it was worth the effort.

Tripp grabbed him before he could make his escape. "If she wasn't a Hollywood executive, who was she?"

Roy shrugged. "I don't know. She didn't say."

"You didn't ask? What do you know about her?"

"Why do you care?"

"Because my wife gets to come to the next meeting while I'm home with the baby. The more gossip I can get, the more she'll have to find out, and whoever has the best gossip at the end of the week doesn't have to make the next batch of mashed carrots and peas."

"You're in a gossip competition with Habibah?" Roy never thought his friend would admit it.

"Yes! Now, what do you know? There's a free order of falafel and pita bread for you if it's extra juicy," Tripp promised.

"And a Coke?" The spices in The Atlas's falafel made his mouth water, but they also made it burn.

"Fine! Give me details."

"Her name was Lucy. Sandy-blonde hair. About

forty. She's going to be in town for a few days at least on a work trip. She likes lime margaritas on the rocks." Roy couldn't think of a way to describe the humor she'd infused into their short conversation, or her congenial smile.

Tripp's head dropped. "Useless. You're useless! That's worth a pita chip at most."

"Look, I'll get more details the next time I see her and send them to you directly, so you can stay ahead of your wife."

"You'd better, or I'll come to karaoke night at your place and then everyone will be sorry."

"Tomorrow. I'll update you tomorrow," Roy promised. Unless Lucy showed up again. Then he'd abandon his friend without a second thought for the chance to get to know her a little better. Opportunities like that didn't happen in Holiday Beach. He was going to grab it with both hands.

CHAPTER 4

THE GOOD NEWS was that Lucy would get to forgo her evening trip to the gym. Tromping through heavy, thigh-high snow was a full-body workout in itself. She'd made several circuits around the exterior of the Dew Drop Inn, examining and recording everything she saw. Her list was exhaustive, and she was exhausted, mentally and physically.

She had another list she usually did for the property grounds, but that would have to wait until the world wasn't under two feet of snow. She didn't mind; she'd found enough to keep her busy for weeks, and that was just on the outside. The inside was likely worse. She didn't even look at the pool or the snow-covered deck around it.

Lucy slowly waded through the last snowbank to the hotel's front doors when she ran into the first person she'd seen all afternoon. Brooke was headed out, with her mom-sized purse over her shoulder and her car keys in her mittened hand. "Hello, Ms. Callahan. How are you?"

"Like you, ready for the workday to be over. And call me Lucy, please."

"Can I do anything for you before I go?"

"Yes." Lucy grimaced when the head housekeeper frowned. "No, nothing like that. I know you're done for the day. I'm soliciting suggestions for places to eat in Holiday Beach, if you have a minute."

Brooke's face brightened. "That's no problem. We have lots of restaurants for a town this size, although some of them are only open during tourist season." She shifted her purse on her shoulder, and Lucy saw an elbow or knee pad sticking out of the top of it. "What are you in the mood for?"

"Anything, but mostly restaurants that serve supper and offer takeout."

"We have all the usual fast food places and franchises. In the morning, if you're a coffee addict like me, I recommend By the Cup. It's an indie place. They have breakfast food too, like cinnamon buns and egg pockets to go. Then there's Colombo's, which has the best Italian and pizza place around. The Farmhouse Table has traditional American food, breakfast through supper. I really like the Atlas Restaurant. It opened a few years ago and they're quite popular. The owners describe the fare as "eclectic." I call it delicious."

Lucy was happy to hear of private restaurants. They usually offered a nice break from the standard fare she found everywhere. "What do they serve?"

Brooke laughed. "Everything! Tripp Turner was a Navy SEAL until he was injured, and he was posted all over the world. He moved back to Holiday Beach a couple years ago with his wife Habibah, who's from Egypt. Their menu is constantly changing." She shook her head, as if dismissing her own comment. "That's not right. Meatless Monday is always on, but the daily specials can range from chicken curry to vegetarian Pad Thai to seafood paella. It's all good, but you never know which corner of the world you'll experience when you walk through the door."

"With that description, it's going to be my first stop. Thanks!" Lucy said. She hadn't expected an international variety to be available in such a small town. "I appreciate it."

"No problem. Really. If you need recommendations for any other businesses in Holiday Beach, let me know. I'm a born and bred local. If I don't know it, I know somebody who will."

"I appreciate that. I'll be sure to take advantage of your offer." Having a local on her side would save Lucy tons of time once she had a complete list of what had to be done. It had been a while since she'd worked on a property in a location so far from a metropolis. She'd forgotten that small businesses had a bigger impact on local economies outside of the big cities. Considering where she was, she could earn a considerable amount of good will for the hotel for when the next manager arrived. "I'll let you get to..." she pointed at the pads, then thought for a minute, "your daughter's volleyball practice."

"Go Wildcats!" Brooke said. "I'll see you tomorrow."

She headed to her car, and Lucy was left alone on the steps. She shook herself like a dog, trying to rid her coat and boots of the sticky snow pellets that had attached themselves to her during her inspection.

"Hello there!" another voice called to her from the almost empty parking lot. A deep voice attached to a large man she didn't recognize.

"Me?" Lucy asked.

"Yes. Good afternoon to you." The man pulled down the scarf covering his face. Then she got a good look at his dark chocolate-brown hair and eyes. He was a handsome interruption. "Hi, Margarita Roy."

He laughed, and Lucy was thrilled to discover he had a dimple. "Or plain Roy, but I'll take it," he said. "Were you doing laps around the inn, through the snow?"

"It feels like it." He wasn't far wrong. She'd examined the roof, checked out all the windows, looked for damaged siding, and counted missing shutters, and each inspection had to be done from a different angle. She'd definitely got in her ten thousand steps for the day.

"I thought the hotel had a private gym. Was it closed?"

"Why would I want to work out inside, where it's warm and dry and I wouldn't have to wear seventeen layers of clothes? That's too easy," Lucy joked.

"I'll remember that," he said. "What are you up to now? Going to work?"

"I'm done for now, but I'll probably work on a report this evening in my room after supper. The housekeeper recommended a place called the Atlas Restaurant, so I'm changing, then heading out. Have you been there?" Not that she doubted Brooke's recommendation, but she needed a reason to stand outside and talk to Roy a little longer. He'd been friendly the night before, and even in the cold his smile was warm and inviting.

He didn't seem to mind the cold either, since he shifted his weight and assumed a comfortable stance. "That's a very good choice. A friend of mine runs it. I'd go with you if I could, but I'm just starting my shift. Try the roasted Brussel sprouts with the garlic aioli. I kid you not," he said.

"Maybe next time?" Lucy hinted, hoping she remembered correctly that Roy hadn't been wearing a wedding ring. She was going to be in Holiday Beach for a while. A dinner date would be something to look forward to. After all, a woman could only handle so many classic movies on cable before she went squirrelly.

"That sounds like fun. We'll have to do that while you're in town. I'd recommend either the Atlas or Colombo's. Did Brooke tell you about them?"

"She said it had good Italian."

"She undersold it. It has great pasta and even better pizza, and a decent wine list. I'm a bartender, so I know about such things," he said with a dead serious tone. He lifted his nose into the air. The gesture had her worried about his ego, but only for a few seconds. Then he burst into laughter and held his gloved thumb and forefinger a couple inches apart. "I know a little about wine, but everything they offer is good."

"Then I'll expect you to be able to pick the perfect red when we go there."

"I promise you can get the owner to double-check my selection." A car door slammed behind them, drawing Roy's attention. "Emily's here. I have to open. Why don't you come by after supper and we can make that date?" he suggested.

Lucy ducked her chin beneath her scarf, so he couldn't see her grinning like an idiot. She liked people who came up with an idea and then followed through. She especially liked it when the person was Roy and the idea was their first date. "I'll do that."

Her assignment in Holiday Beach might not be a complete disaster after all.

CHAPTER 5

ROY WAS ALREADY in a bad mood after an unwanted, unreturned call from Harlan Longfellow's lawyer's office in Boston. Now he knew something else was up when Sheriff Aaron Gillespie walked into the bar. The dart league played on Thursdays, and the sheriff didn't come in during the week otherwise. So when his lanky friend took a stool at the bar, Roy set a coaster in front of him. "What brings you in tonight, Aaron?"

"Nothing special."

"You're a terrible liar. You always have been." Roy had known Aaron since grade school, when the scrawny transfer student had stolen his crown as king of dodgeball. Despite that rocky start, they'd become quick friends. They'd even kept in touch when Aaron moved to Minneapolis to get his criminal justice degree and go to the police academy. Roy had stayed behind, commuting to Duluth to get his business diploma from the local community college.

"If I'm such a bad liar, why aren't you playing poker with us this weekend?"

Roy reached for a pint glass. "I'd feel guilty taking all your money," he said. "But not too guilty, because my muffler's been making noises. Expensive ones." He set the full glass in front of the sheriff. "Three fifty."

"I didn't order that."

"Consider it payment for whatever you came for tonight." Roy was glad it was a quiet evening, although Tuesdays normally were. It gave them time to talk. "Is everything okay with Trevor?"

"I'm holding his driver's license and his car keys hostage. He's at home with an algebra tutor at the moment. That kid is going to drive me crazy. But he's not why I'm here."

Roy didn't take the bait.

"Tripp told me there was a new guest at the Dew Drop Inn. A single lady guest. I'm here in a semi-official capacity to make sure she's not causing you any problems." He tapped the badge pinned to his shirt as he spoke.

Roy rolled his eyes. "How could she cause me problems? Is she doing donuts in the parking lot?" He had other questions too. Like why was everyone interested in this woman, and why they did they keep coming to him when they wanted to talk about her? Lucy had been in his bar once. Nobody else knew about his conversation with her in the parking lot that afternoon, and despite his invitation, she hadn't come in to discuss dinner. It was a shame she wasn't interested. He thought he'd picked up on a vibe, but he must have been mistaken.

"Emily said she was in town for business, but nobody knows what business it is. She hasn't spoken to anybody around town. Don't you think that's strange? Coming to Holiday Beach 'on business' and then not doing any business?" the sheriff asked.

Holiday Beach was small, but it wasn't that small. Aaron had better things to do than investigate the stranger in town. Unless he was interested. Lucy was their age, single, and pretty; Roy had no doubt Emily had also passed along those facts. Aaron could be here to check her out if she put in an appearance.

"There's this new invention called the internet. Maybe she did her business online. Maybe she took the day off. Maybe somebody went to the inn to see her," Roy said. Although he doubted that last one. A local car pulling into a hotel's parking lot in the middle of the day would have drawn all kinds of attention and started rumors that would have spread through town like wild-fire. "I don't know what else to tell you." He wasn't about to give his friend any help. Besides, all he knew about Lucy was that she seemed friendly and had a weird workout routine.

And that she might be interested in a dinner date after all. The bar door opened inward, and a swirl of snow caught on the mat. Lucy stepped through, her red jacket dotted with snowflakes. She'd pulled her navy scarf over her head, so when she pushed it back it left her honey brown hair untouched. She had roses on her cheeks from the cold air, and her lipstick was the same shade of pink.

"Hi, Roy," she said.

"Hi, Lucy. Come in." Roy reached for another coaster. "Another lime margarita?"

"How about a beer?" she countered, pointing at a tap with a stag head on it.

Aaron swiveled on his bar stool, but before he could make his move and force Roy to introduce him, Emily swooped in and saved the day.

"Excuse me, Sheriff Gillespie, can I ask for your help with a customer for a minute?" the waitress asked.

Roy finished pouring Lucy's beer and excused himself for a moment. He didn't like the fact that Emily needed help with a customer, and that she hadn't come to him first. He was proud of the way he ran the Escape Room. He took care of his staff and his customers. "What's wrong?"

"Tiny is insisting he's fine to drive home," Emily told him.

"Tiny's been in here drinking since we opened," Roy said.

"Hence the problem," she agreed. "I figure two minutes from Aaron would save me thirty minutes of arguing with him before I had to call you in, and you'd end up calling the sheriff anyway."

"I'll talk to him. I can call his brother to pick him up," Aaron offered.

"I'd appreciate it," Emily said. She directed Aaron to a big man in the corner, then went back to her tables.

With Aaron out of the way and Emily taking orders, Roy had time for the conversation he'd been anticipating. "How was your supper?" He didn't know how she could not enjoy it, and that wasn't just loyalty to his friend talking. The Atlas had something for everybody.

"It was as good as promised. They didn't have Brussel sprouts on the menu tonight, but I had sesame chicken and some beef and broccoli that was amazing." She offered him a great smile before she took a sip of her beer.

It was good to know they had the same taste. That's exactly what he'd have ordered if he'd been able to go. "I love their sesame chicken night too," he said.

"If you and I were to try that Italian place—"

"Colombo's," Roy said, filling in the blank.

"What would you order?"

He paused. "That's a serious question." Although not for the reasons she might think. He mentally reviewed the menu, looking for dishes he knew were lighter on garlic. "The lasagna is always good, but I can put together a passable lasagna at home."

"How's their chicken parmigiana? It's hard to find a good one."

"It's excellent."

"I assume they have dessert."

"If you have room for it, they have a tiramisu that will knock your socks off."

"A good meal, a good dessert, and a good wine selected by a man who knows about such things. That sounds like a great evening out," Lucy said. Then she took another sip of her beer, set it down, and waited silently, staring at him.

Roy grinned back. Patience was a highly underappreciated virtue.

"Did I hear you talking about Colombo's? Their pizza is amazing, but you have to try the pasta," Aaron said.

Roy noticed his discussion with Tiny had ended with the big man sulking in the corner, but Roy had hoped the sheriff would head out and not horn in on his private conversation.

Lucy gave him a strange look, and Roy realized they hadn't yet been introduced. "Lucy, this is Sheriff Aaron Gillespie. Aaron, this is Lucy."

Aaron retook a seat at his stool, right beside Lucy. "It's very nice to meet you, Lucy."

"Likewise."

Wait a minute. First Aaron gave him a hard time about the new woman in town, and he was putting the moves on her? Roy had seen her first. Besides, they'd already agreed to go out, sort of. "When we go, you can decide for yourself. I have to admit the ricotta and tomato stuffed shells are also off the charts good." Aaron's eyebrows went up, but Lucy simply nodded. Good, let Aaron think he'd swept in and scored a date.

"That sounds great." Then she made a disgusted face and a shiver swept across her body. "Sorry. A clump of snow just slid down the back of my neck. I didn't check the forecast today. I wasn't prepared for snow," she announced, before she gave another full body shiver.

"It's supposed to snow on and off for the next couple days," Roy warned her.

"Then I'm extra glad I did the outside today. Another few inches and some of the places I went would be unpassable."

"What were you doing outside?" Aaron asked.

"I didn't realize you'd been working," Roy added, trying to cut his friend out of the conversation. "Are you a climatologist or something?"

Lucy laughed. "No. If I were, I'd insist my next assignment take me to Hawaii."

"What kind of assignment?" Aaron asked before Roy could.

Roy shifted slightly and rolled his eyes at his friend. It wasn't a competition anymore now that he and Lucy had decided on Colombo's; all they needed to do now was set a day and time. But he'd let Aaron dig for information on his behalf. Roy needed to catch up. Lucy already knew what he did for a living.

"I'm a property maintenance manager. I was outside inspecting the exterior of the Dew Drop Inn, which makes my timing impeccable if it's going to snow. It would have been better to do it in the summer, but I go where I'm sent."

Everything in Roy stilled. Staying at the Dew Drop Inn was one thing, especially if her company had randomly picked the hotel for her. But this sounded like more. "Do you work for an insurance company?"

"No, I work for Longfellow Family Hotels. It's the company that owns the hotel. I organize property assessment and repairs for all their properties."

Roy couldn't believe she worked for that disaster of a company. She looked like she had her act together. Yeah, he knew Brooke Portman worked at the inn as a housekeeper, but single moms did what they had to. Everyone knew Brooke was looking for other opportunities, but while the local economy was improving, it still wasn't great, especially over the winter months. Roy had offered Brooke a job at the bar, but she'd turned him down, saying she couldn't work nights with a barely teenaged kid alone at home every night.

But Longfellow Family Hotels? The company was a cesspool behind the scenes. Every manager he or his parents has the misfortune of dealing with was either corrupt or incompetent, and his family had been dealing with their neighbor for decades. Roy hadn't got the Longfellow vibe from Lucy at all. He must be losing his touch.

He hadn't noticed how the silence had stretched out until Aaron stepped in to fill it. "Does that mean you travel a lot for work? That sounds like fun," the sheriff said.

"It can be. Los Angeles, Nashville, and New York were all great. There were a lot of museums and shows and stuff to do during my down time. It might be a little tougher to find things to do in Holiday Beach but what I've seen looks nice."

"Maybe Roy could show you around town if he has time," Aaron said.

Roy felt a little guilty as he realized Aaron had no idea their competitive pursuit of Lucy had ground to a complete halt on Roy's side.

"You might be better at that, Aaron. My schedule for the next couple weeks is pretty busy. I don't know when I could get away. The poker derby is going to eat up a lot of my time."

Lucy wasn't slow, he'd say that for her. "Does this mean our dinner is on hold?"

On hold. Cancelled. Burned off his calendar with acid. "I think so. Besides, you'll be pretty busy too. The inn is a wreck. It's been badly neglected over the years. What managers there were never did take good care of it." Roy couldn't remember the last time the owner had come to Holiday Beach to check on the property. He would have heard if he had.

Lucy blinked at his harsh words, which surprised him, because the insult was to her company, not her personally, even if she wrongly took it that way. "I'm here for a while. I'll take care of it. Since you share the parking lot with the inn, if you have any problems or concerns, I hope you let me know."

"I've sent plenty of emails to your head office over the years. They'll have them." The door opened, and Roy nodded in that direction without looking to see who it was. "Sorry, I've got to go. Enjoy your beer."

He noticed Lucy leave, but didn't return her wave. He came back to where she'd been sitting to find she'd tucked a bill under her nearly untouched drink.

"What on earth was that, Roy?" Aaron demanded. "She's gorgeous and funny. I thought you liked her."

"I didn't know she worked for Longfellow Family Hotels."

"That's why you shoved her into the deep freeze?"

"She could have stayed to finish her beer." He hadn't exactly run her out of the joint.

"I was speaking figuratively, Roy. You do realize she's just doing her job, don't you?"

The problem with having a friend who was a sheriff meant dealing with someone who was used to dealing with black and white when Lucy fell into a very dark gray category. "She works for a lousy company and that reflects on her character."

Aaron shook his head. "I hope she doesn't judge you as harshly based on your actions today. Because that was cold, and you were a jerk."

"Come on, Aaron. You've met the managers they've brought in over the years. You've had to deal with a couple professionally. None of them have been good people. All they've done is cause trouble. Especially for my bar. The Dew Drop Inn is a dumping ground for bad employees. Do you really think Lucy is going to be any different?" Roy wasn't exaggerating. He'd lost count of the times he'd had to call in his friend to deal with trouble at the hotel.

"I think you're making a mistake. You didn't even give Lucy a chance."

"I'm not going to. If you're interested, feel free to ask her out. I'm cutting my losses." A small voice said he might not be being fair, that he was judging Lucy on past events she had no part of, but Roy ignored it. There was no use getting attached to someone who was going to cut out sooner rather than later and leave him to clean up the mess.

CHAPTER 6

LUCY SWUNG her hammer with more force than necessary as she hit the hanging bracket in the bathroom. Demolition was a terrific way to release aggression, and she had it to spare after last night's debacle. She and Roy had been on the verge of setting a dinner date, and then he reversed direction so quickly she thought he'd left skid marks on the floor getting away from her. She had no idea where things went wrong.

The piece of twisted metal fell away from the wall. Lucy grabbed her small tub of putty and filled in the holes the old hand towel ring left behind. A few minutes later, she picked up the new one and quickly screwed it into place. The repair had been "Pending" for three months and was only a ten-minute job to fix. She was finding a lot of tasks like that. Fortunately, after three hours of non-stop work, she had knocked off an entire page of them. That was a good morning's work.

There were only two other guests in the hotel,

which meant Gloria had been free to help her get organized. The assistant manager sat at the front desk with her laptop on the counter and a stack of work orders beside her. "How did it go?"

"Room Twelve's towel racks are now fully functional. Take them off the list."

Gloria beamed. "You are saving me so much work. How can I thank you?"

"You can tell me when Colombo's is open, and if they deliver. I think a celebratory pizza will be in order tonight, and I know I'll be too tired to cook after a few more rooms."

"They're open for lunch too and, yes, they deliver. Let me treat you to some pizza for everything you're doing," Gloria said.

"I can't let you do that. This is literally my job. Actually, this should have been taken care of for you months ago. You've been dealing with broken rooms and extra stress for way too long." Lucy had already sent a short, initial report back to head office in Boston. Her next one would be lengthy and scathing. "But if you're going to be around for supper, I'll split one with you. I'd love the company."

Lucy wasn't going to be going on any dates in Holiday Beach, that much was certain. But she was always up for making new friends. She'd learned that, although she had to leave behind new acquaintances when she finished a job, she often ran into them down the road at different hotels. It was a fun reunion every time.

Gloria's smile grew even bigger. "That sounds

great. I've been in Holiday Beach for four months and I still don't really know anybody either." She glanced around the lobby, as if somebody might have snuck in without her seeing them. "If we don't get any new guests, do you want to eat in the small meeting room and have a pizza party? They have a huge TV and I have the full Marvel movie collection. I'll be able to keep an eye on the front desk from there."

"Sold!" Now Lucy had motivation for the afternoon. "Unless you want anchovies or artichokes. Then we'll have to reconsider."

"Or broccoli or tomatoes," Gloria added.

"Peperoni and mushroom?" Lucy suggested.

"Deal."

Lucy picked up another stack of work orders and flipped through them. "This is ridiculous," she muttered to herself. She looked up and raised her finger. "I am not blaming you. Some of these date back six months or more. This is unacceptable." She paused and reviewed her last comment in her head. It reminded her of something.

Right. The handsome but rude bartender. "Can you sort these backward, oldest first?" she requested. "Also, Roy next door said he'd made several requests regarding our shared property but none of them had been addressed. Something about the parking lot, I think. We ought to take care of those first. The last thing the inn needs is to get involved in a legal dispute."

It took Gloria till Lucy's next return trip to the lobby before she had an answer. It was mid-afternoon but still light, which was a nice change after months of early sunsets. "I found them," Gloria said. "The concrete dividers in the parking lot are on the Escape Room's side of the property line. Mr. Wagner has filed multiple requests that they be moved."

Lucy could see how that would be irritating but she couldn't see it causing a problem with the parking lot being as big as it was. Even if every hotel room were booked and the bar was full, there'd still be room. "Okay. I'll call somebody in town to get the property line marked, and a tow-truck to move them. Please let me know if Roy has sent any other emails to us. You'd better check with head office too. I don't want to give him any more reasons to hate us."

"Hate us?" Brooke echoed. "Who hates us?" she asked as she came into the lobby with her purse over her shoulder.

"Roy Wagner next door," Lucy and Gloria replied in unison.

The pretty blonde shrugged. "Don't take it personally. Roy's family has been feuding with Longfellow Family Hotels forever. I don't know what started it on their side, but the hotel hasn't done anything to ease tensions either."

"I'm going to take it a little personally. He nearly chased me out of the bar when he found out who I worked for," Lucy told her. Maybe the memory still stung because it was so fresh. She thought they'd had a spark. It wasn't fair that her job had snuffed it out so quickly. She worked for a hotel chain, not Lucifer Incorporated.

"He offered me a bartending job so I wouldn't have to work here," Brooke said.

"Please say you turned him down," Gloria begged. "You're the only other competent person working here."

"I did. I can't work nights since Jordan is only fifteen. It's hard enough leaving her on her own on days when she's not is school. Forget about leaving her alone every single night."

This was the first time Lucy realized Brooke hadn't mentioned a husband. She couldn't imagine being a single mom to a teenager. Lucy looked at Gloria, who gave her a nod. After working together all morning, they were in sync. "If you and Jordan aren't busy, tonight Gloria and I are having a pizza and movie night. Pepperoni and superheroes."

"And mushrooms," Gloria added.

Brooke froze. Lucy didn't know if they'd just made a huge mistake and Brooke was trying to figure out how to make her escape or what. "No pressure," Lucy said.

"It sounds great. Let me call Jordan and I'll let you know."

Lucy headed to the Ruby Suite with another work order in her hand. The hotel had four gem-themed suites, including the one Emerald she was currently in. Hers had been in the best shape. She'd made a note to order new wallpaper for the Diamond Suite, which would go up after she re-plastered the wall where she had to fix a leaky pipe. The Sapphire Suite was missing a closet door, which was also on order.

. . .

After she left the suite's bathroom half an hour later, leaving behind a fully functional shower drain, Gloria informed her Brooke and Jordan would be attending pizza night. "I've rearranged some chairs in there and moved the coffee table in from the lobby. The pizza will arrive at six, which will give Brooke time to get home and give Jordan some homework time, and give you time to..."

Lucy picked her sticky shirt away from her chest. "I'll need access to the laundry room." When the manager flinched, she laughed. "Let me guess. You have work orders for it too."

"A few."

"Bright and early tomorrow," Lucy promised. "But first, a shower for me. I'll see you for dinner."

It took some searching to find a local tow-truck company who was willing to push concrete dividers around a parking lot. Lucy decided she didn't have a week to wait to get an appointment with someone from the land title office to discover exactly where the property line was. Instead, she planned to move them to an area she was sure the hotel owned and leave the parking lot as one large, open area.

If she had a couple more days as productive as the last one, the Dew Drop Inn's minor repair to-do list would be in fighting shape. Then she'd move on to the moderate repair list.

In a week, the lobby, corridors, and public spaces would be ready to impress anybody who walked through the door. At least on the surface. A fresh coat of paint always did wonders. But the spaces people could see were always the easiest fixes.

There was a reason that properties were supposed to be visited on a schedule: so the list of repairs didn't become unmanageable. Lucy was going to have a serious chat with whomever had continually bumped the Dew Drop Inn to the bottom of her list. She still wouldn't be there if it weren't for the special request by the company's CEO. Thank goodness it was a small property. But even with only twenty rooms, she'd already earned a night off. Pizza and skin-tight super-hero suits seemed a fine way to spend it.

The meeting room Gloria set up was huge, but Lucy had to admit it made a great movie theater. Four high backed chairs from the lobby formed a semi-circle in front of the large screen television. She'd also dragged in two end tables from either side of the massive sofa which faced the front window, so they had places for their glasses and pizza plates.

Brooke's daughter was cute. She had the same tall, muscular build as her mother, which wasn't surprising since Lucy already knew she played volleyball. Lucy was thrilled to learn that the young, half-Black woman was also an avid soccer player in the summer. They had a great argument over the changes to the recent national team shake-up as Gloria loaded the DVD into the player.

The two-hour explosion and special effects extrava-ganza ended much too soon, but since it was a school night, Lucy didn't suggest a double feature.

"Maybe we could do this again sometime," Jordan

suggested as she and Brooke pulled on their coats. "But next time Gloria could show me her nail polish collection that she was bragging about." The teenager had been bemoaning how hard it was to keep a manicure intact between her various practices.

"That sounds like fun if your mom okays it. I'll be here for another week or so," Lucy said. "What does Gloria say?"

"The front desk phone rang. I haven't asked her yet."

"Get your mom to ask her tomorrow. Have a good night."

Lucy looked across the lobby and saw the assistant manager nodding absently as she typed on the computer. The easy smile Gloria had been wearing after watching the heroes celebrate at the villain's downfall faded by the second. When Gloria finally hung up the receiver, even from across the room, Lucy could see her hand was shaking. "What's wrong?" she demanded.

"That was a booking. For five rooms. For this weekend. And they want to book the meeting room for a private party. Do we even have five rooms available for guests with all the work you've been doing?"

She understood Gloria's panic. From what she'd heard, five rooms full of guests was more action than the Dew Drop had seen in a month. "We will. I'll at least have all the basics done. I'll knock them off one at a time so Brooke can clean them." So much for sneaking in a second movie in her room. Now she was going to be up rescheduling the next two days and shuffling job orders to keep from disturbing the guests. But business was always welcome, and she'd had to work around worse.

Gloria didn't look convinced. Her brown eyes darted around the rearranged meeting room, and Lucy could see panic beginning to swell. "We've got some time tonight. Let's get everything in here and in the lobby back in place. Then Brooke can tackle them tomorrow and that'll be two of the public rooms off your mind."

Moving furniture was easier with two people. "Thanks for helping," Gloria said.

"You put this together for us. Of course, I'll help."

"This is the biggest booking I've had to deal with since I took over. If the guests leave a good review, it'll help with my application for full manager. I want it. I know I'm young, but I can run this place way better than Roger Lucius did while I was working under him."

Lucy took her first good look at her. Gloria was young, at least ten years younger than herself. The acting manager always wore her thick black hair up when she was working, which when combined with her friendly but no-nonsense attitude, tended to add a couple years to how she looked in general. Lucy had seldom seen a manager in her mid-twenties, but on the rare occasion when she had, it was in a smaller hotel. The Dew Drop Inn was right on the verge of what the company considered a starter location.

Even if Gloria only held the position for a short time, it would look great in her work history. Considering how quickly she'd jumped on board helping Lucy with everything she had to do, even without notice of her arrival, Lucy owed her a glowing recommendation to ensure Gloria got the credit she justly deserved. Together they could guarantee the new booking had an unforgettable vacation in Holiday Beach.

Even if they had the bad taste to use the bar next door.

CHAPTER 7

THE ONLY THING worse than knowing you were behaving irrationally was having other people comment on it. Roy was well aware he'd overreacted to Lucy's revelation. Just because she worked for the corporation that had, for years, harassed his family's business by fair means and foul, it didn't mean she was part of it, or even knew about it. The previous managers were definitely guilty of those tactics, but technically, she wasn't a manager.

Now that he thought about it, the current manager hadn't tried to pull anything since the new year began. He'd had three months of Dew Drop-free angst and had been so concerned waiting for the other shoe to drop that he hadn't remembered to enjoy it.

That was about to change. He had three hours free before he had to go into work, and he was making the most of them. A blueberry waffle and coffee from American Table made an excellent start for the day before he decided to check in on a specially ordered light fixture for the bar.

The Starlight Gallery was set up like most other fine art shops in tourist towns across the country. Paintings and small sculptures from local artists filled the large display windows. Oils, acrylics, and watercolors of every size and shape hung on the interior walls and on wire frames in the aisles. But the Starlight Gallery had one thing the others didn't: a resident stained glass artist with a studio in the back.

Roy didn't blink at the small green shamrocks dotting the store shelves and woven into the frames as he carefully walked down the center aisle. Red hearts had been the decorations of choice the previous week, but a whole new holiday was on the horizon, and they were seizing the new color scheme with both hands.

The white door with the huge window at the back of the shop was open, indicating the artist was in residence. "Sam, are you free?" Roy called.

"Come in. I'm in the supply closet getting more solder." A dark-haired man carrying a spool of thick metal wire walked back to the workbench where Roy waited. Samuel French was tall enough to look him straight in the eye. "Good to see you, Roy. What's up?"

"Just checking on the status of my pool table light." He had ordered a long, rectangular lamp to hang over the pool table in the corner of the bar. He'd thought about expanding the area, taking out a few stools and putting a second pool table, but the dart boards lining the back wall got more play, so it was smarter to leave things as they were. He'd still get to have one of Sam's masterpieces in his bar. "How's it coming?"

"Well enough. I hope you aren't here to ask for an early delivery."

Roy planned to, but it wasn't necessary. "Why?"

"I got a rush order on a window that will cover my expenses for a month. I'd like to knock that out before I finish your piece. I'll still make my delivery date," Sam promised.

"I can wait. I still need Joe to come in and rewire for it anyway." Now he was curious on what Sam would call a big job. "Congratulations on the new commission. What is it?"

"Ms. Callahan came in to order the picture window for the Dew Drop Inn. She made it a rush job so she could install it while she was in town."

"Are you serious?" The words exploded from his mouth. He'd just decided to give Lucy Callahan the benefit of the doubt and she was interfering with his business. "Did she say why she was doing it now?"

"As a matter of fact, she gave me the most recent final notice from the Holiday Beach Chamber of Commerce. Then she offered to pay me for a rush order. I'm not going to turn down that kind of commission, especially since my name was on the notice as the person she had to talk to," Sam said.

"Right. I forgot about that."

A few years earlier, when the town was trying to find a way to put Holiday Beach on the map as a tourist destination, they'd made the unfortunate mistake of hiring a publicity specialist without doing a full review of her references. They couldn't afford the virtual reality tour she suggested they put on the website, or the national internet advertising blitz. But when she spoke about branding the town, the business owners on Main Street came up with something they could do.

Most of them already had stained glass somewhere on their storefront, mostly in the transom windows about the front door. The few that didn't were willing to add a color piece to provide a cohesive look for the area. Then the restaurants on Lakeside Drive, the road skirting the lakeshore and public beach, got in on the look. Now it was mandated that all businesses in town have a stained glass display visible to the public from the outside of the building. "What's the project?"

"The entire round window in the garret. Only the top half was stained glass before. This time she wants the entire piece to be stained glass, with a shatterproof frame put over it to prevent breakage." Sam grew more animated as he got into more details, his scarred fingers flying as he spoke. "Do you realize how big that is?" He threw his hands apart. "Three feet in diameter. And you know there's a light up there because the old one used to be backlit. You'll be able to see it from the street, even if the hotel is set really far back from the road. It's going to hit anyone coming into town right in the face right after they pass the welcome sign. Lucy said she loved the work of mine she saw online, so she gave me free rein on the design. This is going to be a showstopper. I already have a color theme in mind, but I'm refining concepts today. I'll be working overtime, but I don't care."

Roy didn't miss that "Ms. Callahan" became "Lucy" when Sam forgot to keep the commission talk professional. Other managers from the Dew Drop Inn had also been charming before they stiffed local contractors on the few jobs they'd bothered to hire out locally. "Make sure you get paid in advance. You know Longfellow Family Hotels still owes Handler Hardware money from the last time they announced they did repairs on the inn."

"She paid half in advance," Sam said with a smile. "It seems in addition to discovering the outstanding by-law grievances, Lucy also discovered the outstanding invoices file. I think she was headed to the hardware store next."

Great. Now she was trying to buy her way into the community. Roy should warn them to make sure the check cleared before they sold her anything else. "Right. Congrats on the new window. I'll be back to pick up my light in a couple weeks." Provided Lucy didn't bribe Sam with another project in the meantime and get his bumped.

Roy noticed the metallic, emerald balloons in the window of the flower shop, highlighting the white Roman pedestals holding a variety of live, flowering plants, but the ramifications didn't hit him till he walked past the grocery store and the pyramid of Lucky Charms boxes in the window highlighted the "Pot of Gold" sweepstakes taking place inside the store. He needed to get Mickey on the bar's decorations before the weekend. He also needed to come up with a St. Patrick's Day drink special for the next month.

He spotted Lucy before she saw him. Julie Handler, the hardware store owner, was flipping through the paint sample fan deck, pausing to note down whatever Lucy pointed out. He was surprised Julie had time to help a customer herself with the work going on outside.

The decades old, wooden "Handler Hardware" sign was coming down. An electric one leaned against the wall, waiting to replace it. Painters were coating kelly green paint to all the trim, freshening the exterior. It appeared that Julie was following the normal tradition of updating the family business after taking it over from the previous generation.

Spying, no, *observing* through the window, Roy saw the conversation wind up. Julie, a towering blonde wearing a blue smock, gave Lucy a handful of paint chips, which she stuffed into her pocket when she pulled out her mitts. After they exchanged a matched set of friendly smiles, Lucy headed his way.

So he moved.

As Roy dodged out of the doorway where he'd...*paused*...to check out...*the window display*, he accidentally nudged the painter's scaffolding with his shoulder. It shook once, then immediately stilled. He wouldn't have noticed if his sleeve hadn't caught on a bolt. He was five steps down the street when he heard Lucy call a good-bye into the store.

Then he heard, "What the...?"

Quickly followed by a loud metallic clang.

"Grab it, quick!" Lucy shouted. Roy could tell it wasn't directed at him; the order was meant for anyone in the vicinity. He whirled around and found her straining against the scaffolding, pushing with all the strength. All of a sudden, it had gone from vertical to leaning at a noticeable angle away from the storefront and over the sidewalk.

"What happened?" he shouted as he joined her in trying to direct the metal structure back against its support.

"I have no idea."

"Don't let go!" a male voice shouted from above them. "I'm getting off this rig!"

Roy strained his neck and saw a man in paint-splattered overalls directly above him swing his leg over the metal piping. He looked like a spider as his arms and legs landed in different positions as he dropped foot by foot toward the ground. Since the man was working on the roof trim of the two-story building, it felt like it took forever. Every time the painter moved, the scaffolding shrieked with scraping metal, and it seemed to bend a little further. Roy and Lucy heaved again to compensate for the moving weight above them.

Another man, also in coveralls, came out of the store as the climber reached the ground. "Mac, what happened?"

The painter pointed at Lucy. "Don't let go. I need to grab a brace."

Another pipe creaked ominously overhead. Lucy rolled so her shoulders were against the corner, then threw up her hand to hold a board above her head which was beginning to slip. "Hurry!"

The painter and the new guy grabbed a metal

section with clawed ends and ran it from end to end of the scaffolding. They fought to get it attached since the structure refused to stop swaying. Eventually they slipped the brace into place, and the movement stopped.

At Roy's nod, Lucy slowly let go and took a step back. He moved next, and the scaffolding didn't move. "Do you have any more supports you can add?" he asked.

"We'll definitely beef it up." The painter stuck out his hand to Lucy. "I'm Bob Mackenzie. Call me Mac. Thank you."

"My pleasure. Lucy Callahan," she replied.

"Did we get call from you at our office?" Mac asked.

"Quite probably."

"We'll return it ASAP after this rescue."

"I'd appreciate that. Are you okay?"

Roy was about to ask her that. Lucy looked good. A little winded, but she was smiling. Between the strenuous exercise and the adrenaline coursing through his system, Roy also needed a moment to catch his breath.

"Just a little shaken up," Mac said.

Roy recognized Mac's brother and painting partner Doug. "Are you guys going to be okay?"

"Yeah. Thanks for the assist."

"No problem."

Mac turned to Lucy again. "I can't believe you were walking out of the store exactly when I needed you. You should go buy a lottery ticket. You're good luck."

She offered a small smile, looking embarrassed at the praise. "That's sweet, but I'm really not."

"You saved my life. How can you say that?" Mac demanded.

Before she could respond, a clang from above made them all look up. They saw a stream of brilliant green paint arc over the edge of the high scaffold platform. The thickness of the paint meant it seemed to pour in slow motion, but it was fast enough to ensure nobody could move out of the way. It missed Mac and Doug to the left, and him to the right. The full impact of the colored tidal wave almost paused for effect, using the sunlight as spotlight, before it splashed all over Lucy, drenching her ski cap and jacket. The green stream ended immediately, except for one last artistic drop that fell as everyone was about to take a breath. His first thought was that the entire situation was horrible. His second thought was to burst out laughing because Lucy Callahan looked like the star of *Carrie: St. Patrick's Day Edition*.

Before the first chuckle could escape, Roy heard another clang and saw the paint can hang on the lip of the platform for a second before completing its dive over the edge. This time, because he saw the accident before it happened, he was able to reach out with both hands and catch it inches before it bounced off Lucy's head. All thoughts of laughing fled when he realized how serious the entire situation could have been.

"Thanks for that," she said quietly, before everything in a fifty-food radius erupted into chaos.

He nodded, unable to speak from the shock of what had almost just happened.

Mac and Doug were apoplectic at the damage and potential injury their scaffolding caused. Julie came out with a roll of paper towels and a bottle of turpentine. Roy spotted Habibah in the window of the Atlas across the street, her hand covering her mouth as she looked on, shocked. At least two pedestrians had their cameras out, focusing on the still-dripping paint victim.

Roy set the can under the scaffolding where it couldn't be kicked and took two steps back. He didn't have a drop of paint on his hands, or anywhere else. He was completely unscathed. Lucy, on the other hand, was going to make an impression on the entire town, and it was not going to be as favorable as she'd probably hoped. It was an unfortunate way to end her goodwill tour, spreading her money and charm around town in her efforts to get the Dew Drop Inn back on people's good sides after years of being the source of problems.

As he quietly disappeared in the confusion, Roy told himself the whole messy situation couldn't have happened to a more deserving person. But he didn't quite believe it.

CHAPTER 8

IT WASN'T that Lucy didn't appreciate the massive garbage bag from Julie Handler that now held her ruined ski jacket and toque, or the complimentary tarp for her rental car seat, or the bottle of turpentine on the floormat beside her. It was the guilt.

Not hers.

Julie's. Mac's. Doug's. Everyone on the street felt horrible for her. It wasn't their fault. They couldn't have stopped it. She was an accident magnet and she knew it. A little green paint was nothing when compared to being stuck in a car trapped in a sea of manure after a farm truck overturned on the highway, or being locked in her hotel bathroom with only a shower curtain and her cell phone, and calling for help only to have the fire department show up.

Strangers called her "Lucky" Lucy Callahan because they benefited from her presence, but those who knew her knew the truth. She wasn't lucky by any definition of the word.

That truth seemed to be holding when she arrived back at the Dew Drop Inn and saw...nothing. The concrete dividers were in exactly the same places as when she'd left that morning. As she carefully tiptoed through the lobby, hoping desperately that she didn't leave a trail of green paint behind her like some kind of slug, she didn't see any sign of her construction supply delivery either. Her day was going from bad to worse.

"Lucy, you would not believe what happened," Gloria said before she got a good look at her. Then she shrieked, "What happened?"

"There was a shaky set of scaffolding and a runaway paint can. I need to get cleaned up. Can your news wait?" Lucy would have crossed her fingers, but the tacky paint would have glued them together permanently.

"Of course. Do you want me to bring some extra towels up to your room?"

"Only brings ones that I can destroy." Nothing was leaving her bathroom alive.

It took an hour, but eventually Lucy no longer resembled a leprechaun. The turpentine did its job. A little too well. She'd also removed a section of her hair color, leaving her with a few locks liberally streaked with gray that the highlighting used to hide. Not only did her hair look like straw, not even the hotel's signature green tea soap could eliminate the chemical stink clinging to her.

"On the plus side," she said to herself as she pulled her still damp hair through her ponytail holder, "ski jackets are on sale right now because it's the end of the season. Maybe I can find one my size that I like." Lucy had others back in her apartment in Boston, but it made more sense to purchase a cheap replacement than pay to ship an old one out and freeze in the meantime. There was no upside to losing her favorite sneakers or her second best carpenter pants. With the guests arriving the next day, she didn't have time for shopping, especially when it meant driving to the next large town if Holiday Beach didn't have what she needed.

Gloria waited behind the desk, a stack of papers at her elbow. "I still have news for you, but I think I want to hear yours first."

"I already told you," Lucy said. Her public humiliation was likely being talked about all over town. The last thing she wanted to do was relive it herself. "What do you have?"

When Gloria handed her the top message, Lucy noticed she'd changed her nail polish to a deep purple from the lilac she'd been wearing the night before. That kind of paint she could appreciate. "Tom's Tows will be here at two to move the concrete things in the parking lot."

"Excellent. I thought he stood us up."

"There was an accident on the interstate so he's running late, but he'll be here. Next up is Mackenzie Brothers Painting. They called fifteen minutes ago to say they'd be interested in giving a bid to repaint the exterior." Gloria have her an admiring look. "They're highly recommended but they never returned any of my calls. What did you do to them?"

"I stole some of their green paint," Lucy replied in a dead pan.

"Oh," Gloria said in sudden understanding. "They'll be here before dark. Then I took a call from Mr. Fredericks. His party wants to organize a surprise dinner at The Atlas, with drinks at the Escape Room first. He has a ton of excursion booking requests and all kinds of stuff."

"They want a party at the bar?"

"Apparently, Roy Wagner has something on his website for parties, and they want one. I guess I'll have to find time to go over and try to book it for Saturday night. Can you cover the desk for a while? The phone's been ringing off the hook. Exactly how many contractors have you booked?" Gloria exclaimed. "Seriously, I've lost track."

She could appreciate the other's woman's frustration. Lucy could, and did, handle a lot, but being good and efficient at her job sometimes meant not doing the job herself. She raised a hand and started ticking off fingers. "The eavestrough people to clean out the gutters and fix the loose brackets. The repair people for the washer and dryer. Tom's Tows for the parking lot. The tree removal company for the two dead spruces out back. The hardware store delivery."

Gloria gasped. "You didn't mention the hardware store."

"That's new." Lucy raised her other hand. "Sam French will be here in the next day or two to take some measurements for the replacement stained glass window," she said. "There may be more."

Gloria was already pulling extra hours since the new manager hadn't arrived yet. She should have a full staff helping her instead of doing everything herself. That didn't include all the extra work Lucy was piling on her. She could take this off Gloria's plate, but it meant dealing with *him*. Lucy took a deep breath. "I could run over and talk to them. Him. Roy. Or his staff," she added brightly. There had to be other employees there she could talk to.

The pinched look on Gloria's face eased. "That would be great."

A loud rumble from outside ended their conversation. Lucy pulled on her second sweater and stepped outside to see an old blue tow truck idling in front of the inn. The driver came over and introduced himself as Tom Latt. After a brief tour of the parking lot and a short explanation, he set to work.

Since she was already outside and cold and the bar was steps away, Lucy put one foot in front of the other and forced herself to walk through the door which was now bearing a shamrock wreath. The warm, coconut-scented air did nothing to ease the tension in her shoulders. There were a couple of men sitting in the corner, and a familiar woman behind the bar watching a medical drama on a television Lucy hadn't noticed before. She approached slowly, gauging the bartender's reaction with each step.

"Welcome to the Escape Room. I'm Emily. What can I get for you today?" The young Black woman in the Hawaiian shirt was nothing but friendly, giving Lucy confidence to start her conversation.

"Hi, I'm Lucy Callahan. I work next door at the Dew Drop Inn, and I'd like to talk to somebody about booking a party like it says on your website." The last time she'd been inside the building she'd headed straight to the bar. This time she took a moment to look around. There was an area with a pool table and a wall full of dart boards at one end, and a dance area in the opposite corner. Along the far end was a half wall with wooden spindles stretching up to the ceiling. She couldn't see the space behind it, but it was the only place she could see which could be closed off.

"We can absolutely help you with that. What day did you want to book the escape room?"

"I know it's short notice, but Saturday."

"You're lucky. It's free." The rest of Lucy's stress evaporated as she pulled out the list of requirements Gloria gave her, and she and Emily got down to business. She was surprised to learn they had an actual, themed escape room. She assumed the bar name came from escaping the winter cold. But no, they also had a room in the back where they ran a "Murder at Sea" one-hour event.

Lucy worried she might have offended the bartender when she got distracted by the show playing in the background. Then Emily paused to watch with her. "I love this episode," Lucy said.

"They should have brought Marissa Morgan's character back to guest star in season three. She's fantastic."

"Right?" The actress was tragically underrated, despite her Gabrielle Union energy and Kerry Washington emotions.

"I can't wait to see her new movie, and I hate horrors."

"Me too!"

Bonding over their good taste in Hollywood A-list stars eased the rest of their negotiations. It didn't take long to arrange everything Mr. Fredericks requested, leaving both women happy with their plans.

Lucy bumped into Roy on her way out. He smiled for a scant second before his face returned to stone. "Can I help you?"

"No. I'm done. Have a good day." She wasn't going to thank him again for helping her hold the scaffolding, or for catching the paint can before it hit her head. He didn't acknowledge her the first time. If he wanted to take his vendetta about her employers that far, she wouldn't waste her time or energy on him either.

CHAPTER 9

ALL HE WANTED WAS a fresh jar of corn nuts and a twelve pack of cola to get him through the double-header hockey games being televised on his upcoming night off. Roy still had to

make it through the weekend, but after that it was corn nuts, microwaved hotdogs, and cola till midnight.

He could be at Colombo's having a nice pasta dinner with Lucy but that was off the table now. They'd hit it off so well before they started talking about work. But her employer wasn't something he could get over. Longfellow Family Hotels had been, was, and would always be bad news to a Wagner.

It was worse this time because she was sneaky about her evilness. Letting him win their longstanding parking lot dispute. Following up on the Chamber of Commerce complaint. Not letting Julie Handler's painters fall to their deaths. It was all a ploy to lull them into false sense of security before she struck.

And she was lulling everybody. Lucy Callahan

probably had the grocery store clerks under her thrall too, he thought as he saw her coming out of the store with an overflowing recyclable bag in one hand, and her wallet in the other. Her head was down as she tried to jam it into her purse, which was probably why she didn't notice the large patch of ice in front of her.

He didn't call out a warning because there hadn't been time. Her feet went up, her arms went sideways, and her butt dropped like a rock to the sidewalk. He heard the impact from across the street. It had to hurt.

In the next breath, he knew he'd been right. Three different people ran to help her up including his own traitorous bartender. Emily explained what Lucy had booked the night before, and since the end of February wasn't a busy time, the game room she'd rented was available at the last minute. The only reasons he hadn't cancelled the booking was because the bar needed the money and the customers shouldn't be punished for having the bad judgement to stay at the hotel next door. Emily had to be polite to get the booking. But that was in the bar. Not out here in public.

"Roy!"

Now that Emily had called attention to his presence, he was obliged to help, or he'd look like the bad guy. Not that Lucy had done so when he'd helped with the scaffolding, but he hadn't given her a chance then either. "Is anything broken?" he asked as he approached.

Lucy's eyes were glassy, but he gave her credit for trying to laugh it off. "Only my pride. Thank goodness

I decided not to get eggs on this trip. I'm not worried about the corn nuts. They're indestructible."

"You like corn nuts?"

"No! I like my teeth. Guest request," she said as she tried to heave herself to her feet. The ice under her boots didn't cooperate and she went down again. This time the tears escaped, and he wasn't so cruel as to let her be in that much pain.

Roy braced one foot on a clear patch of sidewalk and placed the other in front of Lucy's boot. When he offered her his hand and pulled. She made it all the way to her feet. This time when she slipped, he was prepared to grab her and move her off the ice. "Wow. Thanks. That's rougher than a ride at Universal Studios."

"Yeah." Roy swore his brain stopped working when he got within ten feet of Lucy. Even the suspicious parts. He didn't say "You're welcome" or "I'm glad you're not hurt." Instead what came out was, "I hope you didn't buy the last of the corn nuts."

"No."

Emily, who'd crouched to gather Lucy's spilled groceries, handed the bag back to her. "Here you go, Lucy."

"Thanks, Em."

She was calling his bartender "Em" now? And it seemed she wasn't done either.

"Here," Lucy said. She handed the bag back to Emily and began digging in her purse. She tucked her wallet under her arm and a glasses case under her chin and stuck her face in the large bag before she pulled out a small square of cardboard. "The store says contest runs till the end of the month. I won't be in Holiday Beach that long. You might as well have my extra cards. Who knows, you might win an instant prize. Yay, free bag of chips."

"Or the grand prize. I'll go visit the set of *Santa Monica E.R.* and Marissa Morgan will be the surprise guest star that week and we'll become besties."

"I'm not lucky enough to win that, but if you do, be sure to give my best to Dr. Angel Eightpack," Lucy teased as she traded the bag for the ticket.

Emily broke open the ticket and gasped. "No way!"

"Did you win a gift card? That would be sweet," Lucy guessed. She was too busy brushing dirt and snow off her butt to see the look on Emily's face, but Roy didn't miss it. The last time his bartender looked like that, she'd gotten a callback to an audition in Minneapolis.

"Cash prize?"

"The grand prize," Emily said with a stutter. "I won the trip for two to Hollywood to attend the filming of an episode of *Santa Monica E.R.* I won!"

He waited for it. Almost two years of working with an actress in training meant he knew what was coming next.

"I won!" she screeched. "I'm going to Hollywood. I need to call my agent."

There it was.

"But no, I can't." There was a dramatic pause. Then a sniffle. Roy expected that too. Emily sighed deeply, then lifted her chin in a brave but tragic heroine movement. "It's your ticket. You won."

Now true colors would emerge, and he'd be stuck consoling his bartender about a lost trip to the place of her dreams. Even worse, she'd rightfully refuse to work at Lucy's party, which meant *he*'d have to—

"No way. I gave it to you. It's your winning ticket now." Lucy smiled at her, and gently pushed the proffered hand away. "I'd sign my name on the back of that quickly. You don't want to lose it."

"I bet they have a pen inside. Be right back." Before she could blink, Emily hugged her tightly and then vanished.

Lucy waited till Emily was out of sight before her smile faltered. "Dammit."

"I thought you said you never win."

"I didn't win. Emily did."

"But if it was your ticket—"

"It would have said, 'Sorry, please try again.' It only had a prize on it because I gave it away," Lucy said.

"That's not how prize tickets work."

"It is when I handle them," Lucy insisted.

It was like she was trying to annoy him. "It was nice that you let Emily keep it." There was still a chance she could approach Emily later in private to get it back.

"Of course, I let her keep it. I said it was hers when I gave it to her. I'm not going to take it back because she won a prize. Wow, you really do think I'm pond scum because of where I work, don't you?"

He did, but...

"I'm a good person. I'm proud of the work I do for

Longfellow Family Hotels. I have been nothing but professional and responsive since I set foot in Holiday Beach. I'm ensuring the Dew Drop Inn is up to all town and state by-laws and codes. Where possible, I'm hiring local contractors and ensuring money stays in the community. Whatever your problem is, Roy Wagner, it isn't with me, so find some manners or stay out of my way."

She was halfway to her car before her stunning barrage of words wore off. Roy hadn't been so thoroughly reamed out since he'd been a teenager who tried to snag his father's car keys after downing a few beers with his buddies after a high school football game. And, like his mother, Lucy managed to make him feel like a worm without swearing or raising her voice. It was an impressive talent.

He knew it only felt bad because it was true. He'd acted like a complete jackass.

CHAPTER 10

AFTER SEVERAL DAYS of quiet in the hotel, the
bustle in the lobby was a welcome noise. Three new
cars in the parking lot doubled the usual number, and
the trailers they towed carrying a variety of snowmobiles made the lot look extra full. Gloria waved from
behind the front desk and continued processing rooms.
There were three distinct age groups of guests: a couple
slightly older than Lucy in their early fifties and
another their thirties, an older man and woman, and a
younger pair in their twenties. All of them were
laughing and joking about being glad to take a trip
"south" during the winter.

"You're Canadians," Lucy exclaimed.

Two of them, the oldest woman and the youngest
man, had the same brown eyes. "We are."

"There's not a lot north of Holiday Beach.
Welcome to the Dew Drop Inn. You're the Fredericks
group," she guessed.

The young man stepped forward. "I'm Dan Lewis.

Ben Fredericks is my soon-to-be stepfather, if this weekend goes well. Are you Lucy? Gloria said you were the one to talk to about the party tomorrow."

She gave Dan the details she'd worked out with the bar, then gave them directions to the American Table, which was on the other side of town from the Atlas Restaurant. Dan insisted they couldn't risk their cars being seen.

She waited till they were all on the way to their respective rooms before she approached the desk. "Was everything okay?"

Gloria and Brooke had gone over the rooms as soon as Lucy let them know they were done. The freshly painted bathroom wall in room twelve had been wet three hours earlier. But the Ruby Suite and the three other requested rooms had been in usable order for the expected guests. Tomorrow would be another busy day in case any of the others were needed. By the end of the week, half of the rooms would meet Lucy's standards. Another week should take care of half of the rest, which needed a lot more work. The third week would wrap up her stay in Holiday Beach.

She wasn't too upset about that. Gloria and Brooke were great, and the few townsfolk she met were nice enough, but she hadn't seen anything in this northern resort town to make her want to stay.

Lucy awoke to laughter in the halls, which was a nice change from emergency phone calls. She put in a full day, but at the end of it was happy to scratch several items off her to-do list. Half a dozen dangerous trees were now on their way to be somebody's firewood, and the hotel no longer had rotting branches threatening its roof or power lines. The parking lot was in order. She'd completed repairs in another room. And the painters had arrived and given her a quote that had almost put her in shock. But it was a necessary blow; the exterior gave people their first impression of the Dew Drop Inn. A fresh paint job would be vital for turning the Dew Drop Inn into the charming, quality inn Lucy knew it could be.

Her bosses knew it too. They must. It had to be the only reason they'd approved her budget for repairs on this old place. After years of neglect and skating by on building codes, she assumed her instructions to bring it up to Longfellow Family Hotels standards meant they were preparing it for the new rebranding rollout the following year.

She was on her way out to pick up a late supper for the night when the Canadians trooped into the lobby. There was a fifth couple she didn't recognize. The woman was about her age with short light brown hair the same shade as her own. The man was older, with salt and pepper hair, and a great smile which he sent in her direction. "You wouldn't be Lucy, would you?"

"I am. Is there a problem with your room?"

"It's fantastic. My fiancée loves the view of the lake."

"Mr. Fredericks, I presume." The way he hit *fiancée* let her know he was enjoying using the word, and the unexpected giggle from the woman behind him said she enjoyed hearing it.

"I wanted to thank you for helping Gloria with the

arrangements. We're heading over to the Escape Room now. Won't you join us?"

She noticed they all wore boots and sweaters, but no jackets or scarves, despite the temperatures hovering twenty below freezing. Then again, they were Canadians, and it was only a minute's walk across the parking lot. "Thank you, but that's a family affair, isn't it?"

"It's a party, and you're invited."

The woman stepped forward, hand out. "Hi there! I'm Jilly Lewis. I had no idea Ben was arranging this engagement party weekend, but the more the merrier. He's been bragging about the Brussel sprouts at the Atlas for months, and it lived up to the hype. I can't wait to see what he has planned for tonight." Jilly linked one arm through her fiancé's and her other through Lucy's and led them out the door.

Roy was waiting when they all walked through the door. She nodded at him without saying a word, and he introduced himself and draped leis over their heads. He led them to the party room in the back. "You're partying with your guests?" he whispered quietly as the group gave their order to the young man who'd been working the first time she'd been in the bar.

"Jilly caught me on the way out. She's not a woman you say no to."

"Roy, Lucy, come over here and join us," Jilly called. She and Ben stood beside a large bar table covered in bowled glasses garnished with pineapple wedges and umbrellas. "Oh, Ben, don't they look good standing together like that."

She and Roy each took a step in opposite directions.

"Come and toast to our engagement. If it weren't for Ben's last trip through Holiday Beach, we wouldn't be here, so I'd like to do this with some locals," Jilly said.

They both stepped forward. "Lucy's not local," Roy said. Lucy's elbow flew sideways without a conscious thought from her and rapped him sharply in the ribs.

"Must you? In front of guests? And customers?" she hissed. "What is your problem?" But she forced a smile to her face and thanked Jilly for the glass she handed her.

"To true love, wherever and whenever it finds you," Ben said as he raised his glass. He leaned over and kissed Jilly gently before he had a sip.

"Especially when you aren't looking for it," Jilly added. She reached over and pulled Ben's lips down to meet hers and gave him a kiss that had the others hooting and the young, brown-haired man groaning, "Mom, cut it out!"

Lucy cheerfully clinked glasses with the other guests. She hesitated when she got to Roy, but she didn't want to spoil the mood, so she gamely held out her glass.

To her shock, he immediately clinked back, and took a large swig of the bright green margarita slush.

"Pictures!" Dan ordered cheerfully.

Jilly and Ben posed, their leis awkwardly resting against their turtlenecks and long-sleeved flannel shirts. But they were obviously much in love and posed for all their friends. Then Jilly started moving from guest to guest, pulling them into various shots with or without their consent, which was funny to watch until she got to them.

"Come here, you two. We need a picture with our Holiday Beach friends." Jilly sidled up beside her and reached behind her to put her hand on Roy's shoulder, then pulled him closer. Lucy wrapped her own arm around Roy's trim waist in self-defence as they were squished together. Then Ben stepped to her other side so neither could escape.

"Did you know," Ben said, "I only found your fantastic town by accident? On my last trip as a long-haul trucker, I got rerouted through Holiday Beach and it was the most perfect vacation town I'd come across in thirty years of driving. Cute stores where I found great Christmas gifts, excellent food, and lots of trails and outdoor activities. I talked about it so much that Jilly insisted we take our first vacation here. It was worth it. We had a great time on the snowmobile trails today."

"That fresh snowfall was just what we needed," Jilly said. Then she stepped away and gestured for Lucy and Roy to get even closer. "Now the two of you. Our Holiday Beach friends. If we make this an annual event, we'll have to invite you out on our next ride. Do you snowmobile?"

"Yes," Roy said.

"Never," Lucy gritted out between her teeth, a smile still on her lips.

"It's a lot of fun, if you dress for it." Jilly pushed her hands together. "Closer."

Lucy was practically plastered against Roy's chest before Jilly was satisfied. "Great, got it. Thanks! I'll send you a copy. Now, where was that margarita jug?"

"I promise I'll get out of your beloved bar as soon as I can without insulting the paying customers. I don't want you to accuse me of driving off business along with whatever other imaginary offenses you've pinned to my head." She didn't know how long this temporary truce was going to last, but she wanted to be long gone before it ended. Lucy didn't think she could handle another cutting remark. One a day from Roy seemed to be her limit.

He didn't even look at her. "I'd appreciate that."

The door to the party room closed, and a loud click sounded from speakers bolted to the wall. Then a ship's horn sounded, and a woman's voice announced. "Welcome to the cocktail hour on the Spirit of the Seven Seas. We are an hour out of King's Wharf in Bermuda. The captain informs me that there has been a murder aboard ship. The killer must be caught by the time we arrive, or nobody will be allowed to leave the ship. We encourage all passengers to join in the investigation. Good luck, and may you find the killer before they find you. Mwah-ha-ha."

"I'm supposed to be working," Roy protested.

"It's okay. Emily said she'd scheduled you off for the next hour," Jilly assured him.

"How generous of her," he muttered under his breath.

"You two go look for clues over there. The purser has provided the passenger list, with their cities of origin," Jilly said, pointing at four sheets tacked to a bulletin board on the wall.

He let Lucy do most of the discovery, which she appreciated since she hadn't done an escape room before. It was fun, despite the company.

When the murderer's photo was turned over, a key was taped to the back of the frame. The party returned to the main bar room victorious, and Ben ordered a round of drinks in celebration.

Ben approached the happy couple. "Thank you very much for including me in your party. I'm glad you love my hometown, and I'll look forward to a day of snowmobiling with you next winter. I know there are some trails you wouldn't have found today. Local secrets. But I'm on shift tonight and have to get back to work. If you need anything, let me or Emily or my brother Mickey know. Have a good night, folks."

"I didn't realize that other young man was his brother. Why didn't you tell me? I would have invited him too," Jilly said. She gave Lucy a small shove, until Lucy found her butt on a barstool as the men took over the foosball table.

"How would I know that?"

"Aren't you dating?"

Lucy sprayed margarita down the front of her shirt. "Are you nuts? It was a feat of magic that he deigned to be in the same room as me for more than five minutes."

Jilly frowned, and her forehead furrowed as she processed this new information. "Are you sure? Because I got definite vibes between the two of you. I'm never wrong."

"There's a first time for everything."

"I must admit, I'm more used to sensing this stuff at Christmas, but I refuse to believe I'm that far off. Are you sure?"

"I got to town a week ago. I'll be gone in another two, unlikely to come back," Lucy said. Hearing how quickly Ben had fallen in love with Holiday Beach had spurred her to do some more adventuring in the time she had left, but with the Dew Drop Inn not being a priority with the company, chances were slim she'd be assigned here again. She could return for a vacation, but she'd need a better reason than she *might* like it.

"We'll see," Jilly said.

"About me coming back to Holiday Beach?"

"No." And then the confusing, infuriating woman flounced away, dragged by her son's boyfriend to be his partner at the foosball table.

Lucy's stomach growled, reminding her that before she'd been kidnapped, she'd been on her way to dinner. She said goodbye to the players and their cheering sections and promised to see them off when they checked out the following morning.

But her way out of the bar was blocked by two groups of beer-scented men who were arguing over who got to use the pool table next. She skirted around them and found herself stuck in front of two tables pushed together for a rousing game of beer pong. Stepping further to the side, Lucy paused at the entrance to a small hall beside the bar that led into an area marked "Employees Only" when she heard her name.

"Lucy is nice. I don't know why you can't at least

pretend to be friendly when she's doing you favors," she heard Emily say.

"Like what?"

"The parking lot. The window. Giving your favorite bartender a vacation. Employing a bunch of your friends and other locals so they have money to spend in your bar. She hasn't done anything to you."

Lucy heard Roy sigh. From the hall. "She works for Longfellow Family Hotels."

"So? At least she's competent and getting stuff done. That should make you like her more."

"How haven't you heard this story? Don't you know my mother's maiden name?"

"No."

Lucy guessed before she heard the answer. "Longfellow," she whispered at the same time Roy said it. "My dad and his family built this bar so my dad could run it while my mom ran the hotel. They had plans to turn the whole thing in to one big, family business. But Grandfather Longfellow decided that my dad wasn't good enough, so he told my mom to make a choice."

"Resulting in you and Mickey and a bar that hates the hotel next door?"

"Yes. My mom helped designed that hotel. She put her heart and soul into it. And every time I look at it and it being run into the ground, I want to..." His voice trailed off. Lucy imagined him making a neck-wringing motion with his hands. Or worse.

"But Lucy is helping the hotel."

"Why?"

"Because it's her job?" Emily guessed.

"Even if she doesn't know the history, she's a patsy for whoever does. Nothing happens at the Dew Drop Inn that doesn't have my grandfather's fingerprints all over it. She's the harbinger of something terrible. I know it.

"She's literally doing her job. You complain when the hotel was an eyesore. You complain when she's fixing it. What do you want from her?"

Lucy spun on her heel. She didn't want to hear his response. She'd received enough answers that evening. No matter what she did she'd be the enemy in Roy Wagner's eyes. At least now she knew why. She'd do what she'd been assigned to do and get the Dew Drop Inn into tip-top shape. She'd enjoy the town and stay far away from the Escape Room to increase that enjoyment.

And for both their sakes, she'd forget that Roy Wagner even existed.

CHAPTER 11

MAYBE HE SHOULD GO on a diet. Roy patted his stomach and didn't feel much except for the last bag of corn nuts. Not that he needed to lose weight, but every time he went to the grocery store, *she* was there. Buying her two muffins, two yogurt cups and two bananas that she'd have for breakfast for the next two days. By herself, in her room, according to Brooke.

Not that he cared. Lucy had left him alone since the party at the bar. Not that he missed her. In fact, he was grateful for her absence. Without her there to annoy him, he'd been able to get some work done.

Serious work. He almost would have appreciated the distraction.

The registered letter he'd signed for burned a hole in his coat pocket. He knew it was from the same lawyer who'd been calling his house and the bar. He'd ignored the first two notices, but Peggy at the post office called to tell him to get his butt down there and sign for it because the paperwork was more trouble that he was worth. Considering how many favors she'd done for him over the years, Roy moved his butt.

Just because he signed for it didn't mean he'd read it. Like he hadn't listened to the phone messages before he'd deleted them. The law firm's sole client was his grandfather, and Roy had no interest whatsoever in that old man. Not when Harlan Longfellow had washed his hands of his daughter and her family in every way possible, rebuffing all attempts at a reconciliation. He hadn't been around when Roy's family had needed him. Roy intended to return the favor. The only thing he had to do was put all his concentration on the bar and keeping it going until the influx of summer tourists arrived and...

What was Lucy doing now? Dancing for his attention? She had stopped outside the grocery store door. She pranced from foot to foot, holding her hands and grocery bags high, her short hair bobbing along to her steps. It wasn't until he reached the sidewalk that he saw a compact brown dog with big white teeth snapping at her.

"Barney, no. Down, boy!" A little girl, maybe twice as tall as her dog, pulled at the leash. "I'm sorry, lady. He really likes chicken. Down, Barney."

The mutt left muddy footprints on Lucy's new light blue jacket. He'd seen Julie Handler park in the lot and walk it into the hotel, then saw Lucy wearing it later. He hadn't noticed how blue Lucy's eyes were until the coat brought it out. It wasn't right that a dog was messing it up; she'd just got it.

"Hey, dog. Get down."

The mutt turned and bared its teeth at him. The dog looked from him to Lucy, but before it decided who it wanted to bark at, a car horn blared in the street. It took off like a shot, away from the street, into the parking lot on the side of the building.

The little girl holding the leash looked like a cartoon. Her straight black hair flew sideways, held out by bright pink barrettes, looking like little wings on the side of her head. It looked like she was flying for the first five feet before she hit the ground and her dog began dragging her into the parking lot. The mutt made a sharp turn as it bolted between two parked cars, but the little girl kept sliding. And although she couldn't see it, Roy spotted a car turning into the lot from the street.

Lucy also saw it. She threw her bags to the side as she threw herself to the ground. She caught the little girl's pantleg as her head reached the back bumpers of the parked cars. Horns blared as those nearby tried to warn the car pulling into the parking lot. Roy heard the answering sound of a crunch as metal hit metal.

He was the second to the scene. The little girl was screaming but unharmed. Lucy sat on the wet ground, her back to a car door, winded. She gave a thumbs-up to the barrage of questions asking if she was alright. The woman who got there first was the girl's mother. She sobbed and patted every inch of the little girl to make sure she was in one piece. "I told you to put the harness on the dog for a reason, Shelly. He's too big for you to handle."

Tears welled in the girl's dark brown eyes. "He's not. He's just—"

"He is," Roy said, interrupting. "You're lucky that Miss Lucy kept you from sliding into traffic." He looked around. "Where is that dog? Was he hit by the car?"

The girl glared, then pointed behind him. The dog had circled back to the sidewalk and was chowing down on Lucy's supper. The rest of her groceries littered the sidewalk.

"I am so sorry," the girl's mom said. She grabbed the dog's leash and pulled him away from the trampled bananas and squished muffins. It eventually left its buffet, holding a chicken leg in its mouth.

Lucy looked twice before she accepted Roy's hand. He pulled her to her feet and held her steady at her elbow as she tried to brush off the mud coating her new jacket. "It was lucky you were here."

"Yeah, that's me. Lucky Lucy." The lack of emotion in her agreement was staggering.

"You don't think so?"

She jacked her thumb over her shoulder. He grimaced when he saw what she wanted him to see. A bright sunbeam highlighted the source of the metal on metal sound. The car which was turning into the lot was at a right angle, engine to engine, with a car parked in the lot. He knew that car. "Maybe not so much."

"All I wanted was supper," she said quietly. "I'd be eating it alone, in my room, with a rerun of *Fixer-Upper*, but it would have been nice. Now..." she sighed, "paperwork, accident reports, chips for supper, and trying to find yet another jacket while this one is at the cleaners. What a wonderful day."

The truth was ugly, but he couldn't ignore it. Lucy was right. She paid for the good luck that people around her received with bad luck for herself. He'd seen three instances of it in the last week. He'd sound tired too if every time he did something nice, he was knocked down for being kind.

A realization hit him like a snowball to the head. He was part of that problem. No matter who she worked for, she was helping him, and he was punishing her for it. She was even bringing business to his family's bar, but every time Lucy did something nice for the Escape Room, he gave her grief for it. She was suffering coming and going.

Despite her best efforts, his mother's resentment toward the Dew Drop Inn had been handed down to the next generation, but she'd never take her ire out on its employees. Well, not on the innocent ones like the housekeepers and the occasional competent manager that accidentally managed to get hired. Lucy would have been part of that group.

He was on edge from the unexpected communications from his grandfather, but that, too, had nothing to do with her. It was time, as he was fond of saying to his little brother, to grow up.

Roy retrieved a pack of wet wipes from his truck and offered them to Lucy. She used them to remove the worst of the dirt as she spoke on her phone, first to the rental company, then to Tom's Towing. Ten minutes later, a tow truck arrived, and she and the driver spoke like old friends as they arranged for him to take her damaged car to the local repair shop to straighten her wheel well and replace her tire.

"Come on," he said. "I'm driving you back to the hotel so you can get into some dry clothes, then I'm buying you dinner."

"Will it be poisoned?" she snapped.

He flinched, knowing he deserved it. "No. It's a thank you dinner. I'm sorry for the way I acted earlier. Thank you for saving that little girl. And the guys on the scaffolding. And for giving Emily that winning ticket. She's been talking non-stop about it."

"Are you sure?"

She was wet and shivering and still hesitating before getting into a car with him. He'd done a bigger number on her than he'd thought. He was embarrassed, not by her behaviour, but by his. "I'm sure. Let me apologize."

Lucy gestured at her behind. "I'm soaked."

"I have a towel in the back."

After exchanging insurance information with the driver who hit her and trying to refuse but then graciously accepting a gift card from the little girl's mother to make up for the ruined groceries, they finally got on the road back to the inn. Lucy's teeth chattered despite the vents spewing hot air on her. They paused at the traffic lights, where each post was decorated in large, wire and garland shamrocks. "You know, your town is rather pretty if you ignore the potential death and destruction around every corner."

He chanced a look at her and saw the corner of her

mouth twitch up. She was joking or trying to. "Holiday Beach is not full of potential death and destruction. At least not potential death. The last destruction we had, before you came to town, was two Thanksgivings ago. A float blew a wheel and veered into the post office, but aside from a couple broken legs and two very irate turkeys running down Main Street, nobody was hurt."

"The turkey float had live turkeys?"

"Of course. It was a Thanksgiving float. They were pardoned by the mayor."

"That sounds like quite the parade."

"It's the best one we have."

Lucy stopped squirming and pulling the wet denim away from her thighs. "The best one? How many parades does Holiday Beach have every year?"

"The Thanksgiving one. The Easter Parade. The Homecoming Parade, but that's a little one the high school puts on that has one big float and a bunch of classic cars."

"Does everyone come out to see the same floats every time?"

"Of course not. We have different floats for each holiday and season. They're updated each year. Holiday Beach takes its parades very seriously." The Easter Parade signified the beginning of the tourist season, when people from the city started coming out to open their cottages for occasional weekend trips. By Memorial Day Weekend, the out-of-towners were ready for summer and were patronizing local shops, restaurants, and business. A few daring souls braved the still ice-cold waters of Star Lake to put in their docks in May, but most waited till June, which was when the marina really started hopping. By the time Independence Day rolled around, every cabin was rented, and the local campgrounds were filled. The Thanksgiving parade was the town's big hurrah to send off the year. The local farms and orchards collected their last harvests, the campground closed, and cabins were shuttered till spring.

"It sounds nice. I'm sorry I'll miss them."

"You will?"

"I'm only here for another week or so. Just enough to get the hotel up to code and looking good."

He could have made a comment about Lucy having her work cut out for her, but she already knew that. And it was mean. Instead he went with, "You've been working hard. The outside is looking a lot better."

Her eyes went wide. "Thank you."

He thought she was done, but she must have taking his parade explanation as a desire for conversation. "I've done the necessary repairs. If the Mackenzie brothers can start on Friday like they're hoping to, it'll have a fresh coat of paint too."

"They're painting the whole building?" He made a mental note to stock up on the beer the brothers liked.

"I'm the full meal deal when it comes to property maintenance. No job too big, no detail too small. I do it all."

"The Dew Drop Inn is lucky to have you." So was he. Once she was gone, Roy would be back to his usual animosity with the business next door, but every repair she did improved his property values. That he could appreciate.

He drove her to the inn's front doors. "You know, the ride was enough. You don't have to take me to dinner," Lucy said.

"You don't have anything to eat. And I owe you supper at Colombo's. I'll be back in thirty minutes to pick you up, okay?" He wouldn't mind getting cleaned up himself. The meal could be a disaster, but he didn't think it could be worse than all their earlier interactions. With any luck—his, not hers—it might go as well as he'd hoped when he first met her.

She hesitated before giving him an answer. When he gave her a small nod, her shoulders relaxed a fraction. "Okay. Thirty minutes."

CHAPTER 12

ONCE AGAIN, Lucy was in the two sizes too large jacket she found in the maintenance room. She'd changed into the second of her socializing outfits which she'd squeezed into her luggage. She never needed more than two. When she arrived at the Dew Drop Inn, she'd ironed her slacks and hung them next to her fine, knit sweater that she'd steamed the wrinkles out of. She was glad to have a chance to open the small jewelry case she always carried with her. She quickly donned a small amber pendant on a silver chain and matching amber earrings. A dainty silver watch with a crystal face added just the right amount of sparkle. She didn't have many chances to dress up and be fancy when she was on the road. Most of her days were spent in overalls and work boots, so she appreciated the change of pace.

Part of her, a small but unignorable part, thought this might be a setup. That Roy wouldn't come back, and she'd be stuck in the lobby, waiting until it was too late to call someone for a ride to whatever restaurants were still open.

She shut down that train of thought. Roy had apologized. She would take it at face value, because second-guessing herself was not something she did. She made mistakes, but she made them fully committed.

Her phone said it had been thirty-one minutes when Roy's truck rolled up to the front door again. She waved goodbye to Gloria and darted down the steps. A cold front had blown in, and even the lightest breeze cut like a knife. "I thought Minnesota winters were supposed to be over by March," she said as she pulled on her seatbelt.

"The end of March," Roy corrected. He'd managed to find time to change out of his flannel into a dressy, dark blue button-down shirt that brought out his tan. "Except when they stretch into April. Rarely May." She was glad he joked back. "Is that coat warm enough?"

"It's fine. Hopefully my new one will be dry by morning. I don't want to stand in an open attic window if it's going to be this cold."

"Why are you in the attic? Roof problems?"

"No. Samuel French wants to take a look at the frame for the new stained glass window. He has the measurements, but he wants to be sure the brackets will be strong enough to hold it. I didn't know stained glass was so much heavier than a regular window." She shifted in her seat so she could look at him while he was driving. "What's the big deal with stained glass windows in this town anyway? The inn was getting notices from the Chamber of Commerce, for goodness sake. That seems extreme just to support a local artist."

"People don't have to go to Sam, but he is the best in the tri-state area. As to why, let me show you."

He made a U-turn in the middle of the street, then another right. "This is Park Lane. Further up are the middle school and high school." He pointed out the window. "That's City Hall. Across from it is the library, and then two business on each side of the street. Notice anything?"

Even though four of the six buildings were closed, they all had one lit window. City Hall's was a rectangular transom window over the main entrance, that had "Holiday Beach, Established 1943" on a background of yellow-brown beach, blue water, and light and dark green trees in the background. The filling station had an old-style gas company logo hanging in its window. The library's semicircular window showed a simple open book.

"Here's Lakeside Drive. Most of these businesses are for the summer tourists, but a few are open year-round." Some buildings were dark but even the smallest gift store on the block had a small stained glass seashell hanging in its front window.

"Now we're back on Main Street. You've seen most of these, but you were driving. Take a look at how it all looks to a passenger staring out the window." The street looked picture perfect in the daylight, with nicely kept storefronts and empty planters by the curbs, waiting to be filled with spring flowers. Huge shamrocks and leprechaun hats hung from the old-fashioned lamp-posts. It was small town Americana done well.

She'd driven down this street before, but at night, when all her attention was on the road as she concentrated in the darkness. Now Lucy saw a trail of illuminated pictures guiding her up and down the street. Each was a story in itself: of the business, of the owner, of the area around Holiday Beach. Some were huge, stretching the length of the store window, while others were a small piece, only offering a small part of the overall effect, but still necessary in the continuity of the street. "I think I'm beginning to understand," she said.

"Do you know what design Sam has planned for the Dew Drop Inn window?"

"No. I barely told him where I worked and he yelled something about having the perfect stained glass idea, so I left him to it."

"You didn't ask?"

"I know better than to mess with an artist's vision. My college roommate was a fine arts major, a painter. When you commission art, you may be signing the checks, but you're just along for the ride," Lucy said.

They pulled into a busy parking lot beside a building that had an intricate plate of spaghetti and meatballs in the spotlight above its front doors. Lucy looked around at the neat restaurant. "So this is Colombo's," she said approvingly. "Gloria ordered their pizza, but I haven't been here yet."

"You've been missing out. I think I mentioned they have an amazing chicken parmigiana. Since the dog got your chicken leg, I thought you might be in the mood for it."

"I'm always in the mood for Italian."

They ordered wine and, after a quick look at the menu, two plates of chicken parmigiana. Then, while they waited for their salads, they had the get-to-know-you conversation she thought they would have a week ago.

"How did you get into property maintenance with Longfellow Family Hotels?" Roy asked as he tore into the basket of rolls on the table.

"They head-hunted me about ten years ago from the budget motel I was working at in the Catskills. It was horrible," she said, laughing now at the memory. "The plumbing was a nightmare. I'm not going to get into what it took to keep that place functioning. But my now-boss in Human Resources found my name in some online reviews as the only decent thing about it, and she contacted me for an interview. I handed in my notice that afternoon and have been with the Longfellow group ever since."

"Do you like it?"

"I love it. I love fixing things, even when it gets dirty. I like knowing I left a place better than I found it. The only downside is the travel. I'm always on the road. Head Office calls me their number one trouble-shooter, so get the all the challenging locations. But I've worn out more luggage in the last decade than most people will ever buy in their lives. I'm looking for a position where I can stay in the same place perma-nently. There are lots of cities where Longfellow

Family Hotels have multiple properties, so it's not like they wouldn't still need me full-time. But I'm waiting for a job like that to come up." That wasn't quite true. Two postings had been advertised in the last year, and she'd applied to both, but her bosses told her they needed her where she was. She'd warned them she was burning out, so she hoped they kept that in mind for the next time if they valued her as much as they said they did.

Her story ended when the waiter dropped off a salad which was lightly coated with an oil and vinegar dressing and topped with crunchy croutons and oodles of freshly grated parmesan cheese and ground pepper. But Lucy didn't dive in. From the smells in the air, and the delighted sighs from the diners around her, she needed to pace herself. Especially if she wanted to make it to the tiramisu. "How about you? How did you end up at the Escape Room?" It would be interesting to see what he told her.

"My dad's family opened it before he and my mom were married. It was supposed to be a partnership with the inn but..." She saw a spark in his dark brown eyes before he closed them and took a deep breath. "But," he continued, "that fell through, and my mom stopped working for the hotel and started doing the books for the bar. I started working there as soon as I could. When she wanted to retire a few years ago, I took it over. It's a challenge, especially during the slow season, but it's in the blood."

He left out a lot, but he hadn't lied. "How about

your brother? Is he interested in getting into the family business?" she asked.

"Mickey? No. It's a place to work but I don't think he has any intention of making it a career. I don't think he has any idea of what his intentions are. He's fifteen years younger than me, and some days it seems like a hundred. When I was his age..." Roy shook his head and laughed. "When I was his age, someone my age was ancient."

She laughed ruefully. "Hey there, buddy. I'm right up here with you."

"You make a lovely lady Methuselah."

That was as far as she was willing to push work talk without risking annoying Roy again. Now that they were finally not at each other's throats, Lucy searched for another safe topic of conversation. "You told Ben there were snowmobile trails around Holiday Beach that he didn't find. Are you a big snowmobiler?"

"Yes, in the winter. The local club teams up with the hikers' organization to keep them groomed all year around. I'll go out with a tent, hike halfway around the lake, camp for the night, and come home. It's a great weekend trip in the summer."

She didn't hide her horror. "Camping outside? In a tent? Separated from the bugs and forest creatures by only a thin sheet of nylon? Not on your life! I've never tried snowmobiling, but it sounds like fun. And a hike is great...so long as you can come back to the spa at the end of the day for a nice massage and a glass of wine."

"City girl, huh?" But the comment held no malice.

"One hundred percent. But I was serious about the

hiking. I've even done a couple days on the Appalachian Trail. Short days, but I was there and have pictures to prove it."

"It's gorgeous in the fall."

"It's stunning." She imagined fall here would have a different kind of beauty. It was flatter, so instead of coming across a bluff overlooking a striking vista, hikers would have to tramp through the woods to see all the colors. Minnesota would have more evergreens and spruces, less red maple and yellow birch. Different birds preparing to nest for the winter or migrating south to avoid the cold.

That led into a vacation discussion, which she would have won if it were a competition. Roy didn't have the travel bug. He was content to spend his days off in Holiday Beach or venturing to Minneapolis for a few days. The idea of staying in one place confused her. She'd been on the move for so long she'd forgotten what it was like to be still.

The meal was everything Roy promised and more. For as long as she was in town, Lucy promised herself she wouldn't go more than four days without a meal from Colombo's. She was prepared to replace the gym equipment since she'd wear it out burning off the calorific pasta, but it would be worth it.

"Thank you for a lovely dinner. I really enjoyed myself, Roy."

He cleared his throat twice. "Thanks for saying yes. I'm sorry it took me so long to make it happen."

"We got there. That's what matters."

She didn't know how it was possible, but it was

even colder on the way home. Roy turned the heater to full, but her breath hung in the air when they arrived at the hotel. Still, she lingered in the truck.

"What are you up to tomorrow?" Roy asked.

"The window with Mr. French. Then I have to repaint the ceilings in two rooms, and make sure the new industrial washers and dryers get installed and the old ones taken away."

"Sounds like a full day."

"It will be."

"Well, when you're finished, why don't you come over for happy hour?"

"That's the best idea I've heard in a week. I'll be there." A chance to relax and chat with a friendly face after work as just what the doctor ordered to give her enough energy to finish the job. Because as busy as tomorrow sounded, Lucy knew all the days after it would be even worse.

CHAPTER 13

ROY TRIED to forget about the letter in his jacket pocket. He didn't think about it the previous night when he'd been out with Lucy. He ignored it during his morning workout and told himself he was too busy paying bills to look at it over lunch. But now he had two hours before he had to open the bar, and he could hear it calling to him from inside the front hall closet.

It was thicker than ordinary printer paper, with an embossed header garishly announcing the document was from William R. Truman the Third, Attorney-at-Law, in the Commonwealth of Massachusetts. The flowery introductory paragraph confirmed Roy's initial impression. This guy was going to take five times the necessary words to say something Roy didn't want to hear anyway. Considering the letter was—he flipped to the end—four pages long, he settled in for a long read.

"You have ignored our previous attempts, yadda, yadda, yadda," he read aloud, the skipped through the next three paragraphs where a man he didn't know berated his lack of manners and responsiveness.

"Your grandfather, Harlan Tiberius Longfellow, is an esteemed, highly-respected businessman with his worldwide hotel empire headquartered in Boston, yadda, yadda, yadda," he continued, reading through the various awards and accolades the old man had collected over the years.

Mickey came out of his spare room and headed toward the bathroom, wearing nothing but a towel. "Since when do you get registered mail?" he asked as he paused the in kitchen to pull an orange juice box from Roy's fridge.

"Why are you showering at my place?"

"All my towels are dirty and the washing machine at my place is broken, so I'm using your shower before I throw this towel in with the others."

His brother was his exact opposite. If people got half their DNA from each parent, he and Mickey got opposite halves. The only thing they had the same was their eye color, since both their mother and their father had been brown-eyed. While Roy was average, the kind way to describe Mickey was to say he was barrel-chested. And barrel-armed and barrel-thighed. His baby bro was, to put it bluntly, squat and compact. Not short, because five-foot-seven wasn't short, but it was nowhere near Roy's five-foot-eleven.

Their personalities were equally diverse. Roy picked a goal, planned, worked until he achieved it, and then picked a new goal. It drove him nuts that Mickey picked a goal, then another one, then a third, then dropped the first to pick a fourth while starting to plan how to use the second, which he still hadn't achieved, to jump the fifth, all without actually doing any of the work. The kid was twenty-five years old and had had more jobs than Roy had toes. The only reason he'd kept his job as assistant manager for the last six months was because he was family. Now even that might not save him. It may be the family business, but it was a business and Roy ran it the way he'd been taught by their parents.

"It's from Harlan's lawyer."

"Oooh. Fancy. What does he want this time?"

Okay, they had two things in common. Their eyes, and their mutual distain of their mother's father. "I haven't got that far yet. I'm at the top of the second page and the lawyer is still rambling."

"Let me know if he died and left us anything."

"Besides problems," they said at the same time.

"I will."

Roy heard the shower start and returned his concentration to the letter. "Mr. Longfellow would like to meet you." He paused, then read that line again. "Mr. Longfellow would like to meet me? Me, the grandson he's never been interested in before. Sure, he would. Mickey's right. He's dying." He read a little further. "Mr. Longfellow expects to see you in his office at 3 p.m. on March first to discuss the Dew Drop Inn's association with the Escape Room, and what the bar's new responsibilities would be in relationship to the hotel property. What?" he yelled in the empty room. Did his grandfather really expect him to fly halfway across the country on one week's notice? The old man really had lost his mind.

"What are you yelling about now?" Mickey asked. His shaggy hair draped over his eyes, but it was washed and dried, and he was freshly shaven. He didn't take much seriously but his looks made the list.

"I'm expected to be in Harlan's office one week from today," Roy said, waving the letter.

"I'm sure you'll jump on the first plane to Boston so you don't disappoint old Harlan." Mickey laughed. "Does it say anything else?"

"I'm so annoyed right now I don't want to keep reading. But I suppose I should. There's only one page left." Roy skimmed until he found the only other line of interested. "Mr. Longfellow would also like to discuss matters of a personal nature with me."

"Do you think he knows that he has two grand-sons?" Mickey asked.

Roy wasn't sure if the bitterness in Mickey's voice was from the fact he'd been ignored in the letter, or the fact their grandfather was bothering them at all. "He's probably senile." He pulled the lawyer's business card from the paperclip that attached it to the first page, then balled up all four pages and tossed them into the trash can. "Two points! It's the only thing of value in that whole thing."

"Wait a minute." Mickey fished the letter out of the trash and flattened the sheets again.

"Did you want to save that?"

"No." He disappeared for a moment, then came back with something tucked under his arm. He plugged it and set it down. "You can't just throw away a letter from Harlan." He flipped a switch and the machine began to grind. "You should shred and recycle it." Mickey feed all the pages it at once, and the shredder ground it up like it was starving for a paper meal. "Now that's how you get rid of it."

"That is much more satisfying."

"We'll use it for fire starter later."

Roy offered his brother a high-five. "Even better."

CHAPTER 14

LUCY WAS thankful the new washers and dryers were installed and working. She was going through two sets of clothes a day. But she needed her first set to last a little longer, so she brushed the drywall dust off her shirt and slapped the scraps of paper from her jeans. A quick stop in her room to comb her hair and wash the dirt from her face was all she could spare before she raced to the lobby to welcome the inn's latest tradesman.

Samuel French, with his dark hair and startling purple eyes, greeted her with a smile. He waved off her offer of supplies, telling her he'd brought his own stepladder and toolbox with him. They climbed the first staircase to the second floor, where Lucy led him to the laundry room and the hatch with the collapsible staircase leading to the attic. She'd been up there before to measure the window, but this time Sam was coming with her. A fresh layer of regular dust—sawdust and disintegrated cobwebs and dirt that had blown in through the ventilation ducts—coated her already dirty work clothes.

By the time he maneuvered up the staircase and placed his ladder, he was as dirty as she was. Fortunately, he laughed with her. "Such glamourous lives we lead. All those poor souls in nice clean offices don't know what they're missing."

"Yes, with all their fluorescent lighting and sunlight streaming through their corner windows. They suffer such miserable existences," she joked as they struggled to read Sam's measuring tape in the dim light thrown from the two naked bulbs which were supposed to illuminate the whole area.

It didn't take him long to get his measurements, and Sam happily announce hers had been exactly right. He promised the newly framed stained glass window would be ready by week's end.

"Isn't that awfully fast work? Not that I'm doubting you because I haven't seen a picture of it yet," she added quickly. "But it's such a large piece for the inn, and you had to design it from scratch, plus you probably have other commissions..." Lucy sighed. She was making a mess of things. She was interested in the whole process, but it sounded like she was accusing him of a rush job. It was going to be like the scene in the bar with Roy all over again, but with a new person.

Sam burst into laughter. "If that's what you're worrying about, forget it. I've been dying to work on the Dew Drop Inn window ever since they brought in that horrible one from out of state and slapped it up. I've had a design waiting for years. All I had to do was cut and assemble it. You're going to love it."

"Is that all I get? 'You're going to love it.' Give a girl a break, would you? At least give me a sneak peek. Not as a buyer, but as an interested person."

"No chance, Lucy. This piece is going to be my masterpiece. People will flock to the Dew Drop Inn just for the chance to lay their eyes on it."

"I'll prepare Gloria for the hordes of reservations to come."

"Charge them double. It'll be worth it."

After they returned downstairs and Sam had his truck loaded, he turned to her and asked, "Are you done for the day?"

"I am. You're my last contractor today."

"Then can I interest you in a drink over happy hour next door. It's margarita night."

"I thought that was Mondays."

"At the Escape Room, every night is margarita night."

"In that case, I'd love to."

The bar was hopping when they arrived in the middle of happy hour. They found two recently vacated seats at the bar and had to wait for Roy to get to them.

"Two of your finest margaritas, my good friend," Sam said to Roy after they greeted each other across the bar.

"I take it the window fitting went well," Roy said.

"It's going to be perfect. I can't wait to finish. Then I can return to work on your project."

Lucy's stomach dropped at the casual comment. When she hired Sam to do the window, he assured her he had nothing else on the books and would be able to rush the order. If he bumped a regular client, a local client, for her, she'd look bad. That would go double if it was Roy. "Sam, you said you had time for a new commission. I didn't mean for you to cancel any existing contracts because I was in a rush."

"Don't worry, Lucy. Roy's wasn't a rush, and I'd built in a buffer with his piece. I can finish yours and still get his to him on time." She must not have looked convinced because he laid his hand on her arm. "I promise."

"It's okay, Lucy. I knew he took a break to work on yours. I'm still getting my pool table light on time," Roy assured her.

That was a relief. Not only hadn't she messed up anyone's calendar, but Roy taking the time to be nice proved the previous night hadn't been a one-off.

"Is this a date or a completed piece celebration?" Roy asked.

Lucy was going to say a date, although a casual one, since the piece wasn't completed. But Sam beat her to it and raised his glass. "We're celebrating. Now that I've confirmed the measurements, Lucy will get her window in the next few days. She's going to love it."

"Then here's to new windows." Roy raised a glass of ginger ale before he left to serve other customers.

With that clarification, she relaxed a lot. She and Sam started talking about other places they'd worked.

She rhapsodized about her last job in California, and asked Sam why he smiled when she mentioned it.

"I have a girlfriend there," he said.

"You have a girlfriend?" Roy materialized beside him. "How did I not know about this?"

"How did you even hear me? The music is blaring and there are a dozen conversations going on."

"But none of those are about my friend having a secret girlfriend."

"It's not a secret. And she's more of a girl who's a friend than a girlfriend." Sam made a face, then took a big gulp from his slush filled cup. "That sounds pathetic at thirty-five. She's my online girlfriend. For my New Year's resolution, I decided to join an online dating website. I met someone and we've been chatting for three months."

"Why haven't you gone out on a date yet?" Lucy asked.

"Because she's in California."

Lucy gave Roy a sidelong look. "You have to admit that's a good reason."

"It's a good thing he got your commission then, so he can save some airfare. Once he's done my lampshade, he'll have no excuse not to head to the coast. I'll get to work on drumming up some new business for you, Sam." Then Roy was gone again.

"Lucy, it's been lovely, but I'm getting out of here before Roy kicks the rumor mill into high gear. I'll finish the framing tomorrow and call you in the afternoon or the morning the day after, and we'll set a time to get your window into place." Sam donned a black knit cap and slipped out the door when he saw Roy heading their way with another man Lucy didn't recognize.

Roy's companion wore an expensive gray wool coat, gray wool slacks, and, oddly, a gray felt fedora. Lucy knew nothing of him beside these three facts, but the ensemble screamed accountant with a very active gym membership. "Lucy Callahan, I'd like you to meet Josh Huntington. He's the head of the Holiday Beach Chamber of Commerce, as well as the owner of Diesel Fitness. We have a favor to ask you. Josh, this is Lucy."

"Hello Mr. Huntington. I hope Roy told you I'm taking care of the window that you sent the notices about. Samuel French was just telling me it should be taken care of by the end of the week." Man, these people were serious about their by-laws.

"I'm not concerned with that, Ms. Callahan. What I am concerned about is the Junior Shamrock Baking Championship and our lack of judges. As an outsider to Holiday Beach, you wouldn't have any existing biases or familial relationships to any of our junior bakers, and Roy tells me you'll be available a week from now, on Wednesday night." The man spoke as if she'd already agreed. If she hadn't practiced the same tone herself when it came to contractors, she would have immediately folded to the pressure. As it was, she knew how to play the game, so she waited.

Roy broke first. "I said she'd still be here next Wednesday. I didn't say she was available."

Josh gave him a disappointed look. "Roy, you said you were both free."

"Because I was hoping to ask her out on a date, Josh! Not so you could lasso us into being judges."

Lucy held up her hand. "Hold on. You want me to judge a baking contest? Where, I assume, I will get to sample all the goods, likely multiple times?" Her sweet tooth screamed at her to agree before the offer was rescinded.

"Wait a minute, Lu—"

"That's exactly what I'm proposing, Ms. Callahan," Josh Huntington interrupted. "We have twenty-four contestants."

The invitation to participate in a beloved town event warmed her heart. Even as an outsider, they were welcoming her into the fold. "I'd love to judge your amateur baking contest, Mr. Huntington."

"Fantastic!" The gray man gloated. "We're lucky to have you. We'll drop off a package at the hotel tomorrow for you with all the details."

"Sounds great."

"Our students will be excited to meet you."

"Your cooking school students? I didn't know Holiday Beach had a cooking school."

"No, our middle schoolers. My email will be in the packet. Let me know if you have any questions," he said.

She waited till he was out of earshot before she leaned closer to Roy. "Middle schoolers?" she repeated.

"That's what I was trying to tell you before you jumped the gun. It's the Junior Shamrock Baking Championship. *Junior* as in junior high school. Have you ever tried an original recipe from a thirteen-year-old? I have. The words 'too much sugar' have absolutely no meaning to them."

"Why didn't you stop me?" She did know thirteen-year-olds. Coworkers and friends never ceased to amaze her with the concoctions their children would come up with when left to their own devices. Before Roy could speak, which was how she got into this trouble in the first place, she dismissed her own question. "It's a baking contest. They aren't going to try to gross out the judges, right?"

Roy said nothing.

"Right, Roy? Buddy?"

CHAPTER 15

UNTIL HE WENT LOOKING, Roy had no idea that four stores in town sold ladies' long underwear. It seemed excessive, but convenient as he texted Lucy the list. She promised to hit at least one of them before their lunch date the next day.

Getting her into a pair of long underwear was only the first step. Finding a snowsuit for her to borrow was the second. Thankfully Peggy at the post office came through for him and offered to lend Lucy hers for the day. He dropped the overall-style snow pants off on Wednesday just before he started work.

Thursday finally rolled around. He stopped at the gas station to fill up both his truck and his snowmobile, then headed to the Atlas with a cooler just before noon.

"Got a hot date, Roy?" Habibah Gamal asked. Tripp's wife was terribly shy until she got to know a person. Then she was only mostly shy. Roy, however, had been around for years. At this point, they were good enough friends for her to give him grief over his single status and try to fix it for him. Giving her a glance into his social life was going to earn him lots of good will and treats at the restaurant. It would also put Tripp behind the eight-ball when it came to town gossip, but that was only part of being a good pal.

"No." When her eyebrows rose, he smiled. "I have a cold one. I'm taking Lucy on a snowmobile picnic. Help a poor, bumbling, single man out with a lunch to impress a lady?" he begged without shame. When she smiled, Roy knew Tripp would be buying flowers for a week to make up for not letting his wife know Roy was going on a date.

"Of course, Roy! Come back into the kitchen and we'll prepare a lunch for you and your lady. When are you going to bring her in for a proper meal?" Habibah washed her hands and took over a prep station. Her knife flew as she sliced a chicken breast into thin strips, then layered them with tomato and lettuce between thick slices of homemade bread. Then she filled one of Roy's thermoses with steaming hot vegetable soup, and another with hot chocolate. "Wait!" she said before he fastened the lid. She slipped four cookies into a disposable soup bowl. "You can't have a date without dessert."

He left the truck running when he pulled up to the Dew Drop Inn. Lucy was chatting with Gloria, her winter boots sitting beside a chair in the lobby, when he walked in carrying the borrowed snow pants. "Are you ready?" he asked.

"You bet." She was wearing jeans and a puffy sweatshirt. The collar sticking out from under it left no doubt it was covering another shirt underneath.

"Did you get the long johns?"

Lucy pulled up her pantleg to reveal gray leggings stretching under her sock. "They're very sexy."

"They're sexier than frostbite."

"True." She stepped into the nylon pant legs, and pulled on the rest like a very thick, padded set of overalls. "Yeah, this is definitely sexy."

"I think you look adorable," Roy said. Nobody made snow pants look good, but Lucy did her best. "I'm sure I look equally magazine-cover worthy." He had a full, one-piece snowmobile suit. It was only two years old, so there were hardly any grease stains on it, and the reflective tape on the arms and across the chest still had a good shine.

Lucy wound a thick scarf around her neck and tucked in the ends. Then she added her toque and mittens. "Let's get out of here before I melt," she begged.

Roy led her out the front door to where his snowmobile was already waiting, the cooler strapped to the back of the machine. He would have liked to take Lucy on a ride on his favorite trails past the old Holiday copper mine. But that was a two-hour ride, and she was already stretching her lunch break as it was. Instead, he planned to take her around part of the lake to the Bonfire Bay Campground which was closed this time of year. They had picnic tables near the beach, and while the sand was covered in a foot of snow and ice, the view of the frozen lake from the grassy playground further away from the shore was spectacular.

"Have you ridden a snowmobile at all?" he asked,

while he demonstrated how to swing a leg over the wide body of the machine.

"Never."

"How about a motorcycle?"

"Also a big no." She paused with her hand on his shoulder. "I was on a horse once. Will that help?"

Roy burst into laughter. "Put your feet where I tell you, then wrap your arms around my waist and hold on tight." He braced her boots on the boards and let her find a comfortable position. Although she couldn't see it, his face broke into a huge grin when she squeezed him tight.

"Dashing through the snow, in a one-horse open sleigh," he heard her say under her breath.

"A hundred and fifty horses, but who's counting." Then he hit the gas.

Lucy's terrified scream quickly turned into one of delight. They zoomed behind the inn and through a gap between two spruce trees. Then he veered toward the lake.

The recent snow had padded the trail, and the cold weather had preserved it, giving them a thin layer of cushioning above the packed snow trail. Snowmobiling in March was iffy; sometimes an early spring melt after a winter of poor snowfall left the trails an icy, muddy mess. This year had been decent tobogganing, and with the sunny weather in the forecast, Roy was glad to have one last chance to get out.

Sunlight streamed through the trees, highlighting all the various shades of green and brown against the snow. An occasional rabbit quivered under bushes as they went by, only their twitching ears giving away their location.

The deserted beach was only a twenty-minute ride from the inn. Lucy brushed the snow off the picnic table top while Roy unstrapped the cooler and brought their lunch over.

"Chicken sandwiches, soup, and dessert," he said, handing her a tinfoil wrapped package with a flourish. "It's not Colombo's but it's exactly what we need for lunch."

"All this fresh air has me starving," Lucy said.

She poured the hot soup into the cups he provided, and he did the same with the hot chocolate. "What do you think?" he asked.

"It was fun. I'm glad it was only a short ride for my first time, though." She waved her hand around. "This is amazing. I'll bet it's even better in the summer."

"It is. Of course, in the summer this place would be teeming with campers and their screaming children. Every square foot would be covered with towels and picnic blankets and inflatable water toys. So would the public beach in town."

"According to the records, the Dew Drop Inn has a corner that touches Star Lake. Does the hotel have a private beach?" Lucy asked.

"No. Not even a dock. There's a small, rocky piece of shoreline that technically belongs to it, but all it does is divide the town's beach from a row of lakeshore cottages."

Lucy stopped her nod of agreement in mid motion.

"This sandwich is amazing. Why has nobody told me about these yet?"

"Habibah doesn't put them on the menu. She made it special for us."

"Tell her thank you."

They ate in a surprisingly comfortable silence. Birds returned to the trees once the roar of the snowmobile died. The air was still, the cold wind done for now. "You know," Lucy said suddenly, "I could see myself working in a place like this, if I could find a place that needed a full-time property maintenance person. Or if I won the lottery."

"You could? I thought you were a city girl."

"I grew up in one. And I've always worked in them. Holiday Beach is the smallest place I've ever been assigned to. But I like it here. I like the pace. I like getting to see the same people every day. I like the fact a morning commute takes twenty minutes and not two hours. I like the scenery and all the green." She heaved a great sigh, and he could hear the contentment.

"Maybe you could start looking for a place now, so you have it lined up for when you win. How does a nice lake house sound? We've got some excellent properties around here. Unless you have another place in mind." Roy thought everybody should live in a place like Holiday Beach. It had everything anybody could want. But Lucy spoke like she already recognized that.

"It's already on the list."

"I'm glad. You couldn't pay me to live in a big city. I vacationed in New York City once. I didn't understand the term 'concrete jungle'" until then. I walked for blocks without seeing so much as a tree. I nearly pitched a tent in Central Park when I found it because I so desperate for some nature. I never went back." Almost as bad as the never-ending sea of people was the noise. There was no place to hide from it. Nowhere he could go to clear his head. At home, the worst things he'd hear were cawing crows or a chittering squirrel waking him up at sunrise.

"I loved New York. But if I had to choose, despite the twenty-four-hour restaurant delivery and Broadway and everything else, I think I'd pick a place like this." She tipped her plastic cup and shook out the last few drops of her hot chocolate. "I guess we have to head back. My boss is pretty good about me having an extended lunch hour, but she's insisting I make up the time later. She's a real stickler about that stuff."

They stowed their trash and thermoses back in the cooler, and Roy strapped it onto the rear of the snow-mobile. Then what she said hit him. "Wait a minute. Aren't you the boss?"

"What can I say. It's not easy being me."

They laughed the entire ride back.

CHAPTER 16

ROY JOLTED awake for the third time, the dark sky showing the first signs of the coming dawn on the edge of the horizon. At first, he thought he had another dream about endless snowmobile trails, but the buzzing on the nightstand revealed the real reason he was up.

The black phone was hard to spot on the black wood. His eyes were too blurry to read the number, but if anyone called him before dawn, it had to be an emergency with the bar. "Wagner. What's wrong?"

"What's wrong is that you are fifteen minutes late, Royal Wagner."

It was a man's voice. Old. Growly with a bit of a rattle. And a bigger hint of a Bostonian accent than Lucy's. Even with all those clues, it took him a moment to put it together. "William R. Truman the Third, Attorney-at-law, is that you?"

"No, you ungrateful pup, this is your grandfather."

"Harlan Tiberius Longfellow?" His mother always

said his grandfather hated his middle name. Maybe Roy was still dreaming, and this was a nightmare.

"Grandfather will do. How close to the office are you? I don't hear any street noises. You are on the way, aren't you?"

"The way to where?"

"To my office! You were supposed to be here at eight o'clock sharp. I don't appreciate you wasting my time—"

Now he remembered. The letter he threw away, Mickey shredded, and they burned together in the fireplace. "What do you know? We do have something in common." Then Roy hung up and threw the phone back on the nightstand.

It had been a long weekend. Emily had called in sick both days, and she never called in sick, leaving him and Mickey to handle the Friday and Saturday night crowds with their other waitress. Roy had barely had time to shower and sleep before he had to be back at the bar. He hadn't caught a glimpse of Lucy in days, although she did send him a picture of the bar taken from one of the platforms on the painters' scaffolding. He wondered if he and Lucy could get in one more ride between their schedules.

His eyes closed and he was drifting off when the phone rang again. "What?" he barked.

"I don't know who you think you are, but in my world, when a man has a meeting scheduled at eight o'clock, he shows up on time," the grumpy Bostonian continued as if he hadn't just been hung up on.

"It's a little past seven in the morning and in my world, businesses run from four in the afternoon till one in the morning, so you're calling me at home in the middle of the night. And for your information, I didn't schedule a meeting with you." If he were slightly more awake, Roy felt he'd enjoy giving the old man so much grief.

"Bill Truman requested—"

"Your lawyer sent a letter telling me where to be and when to be there. I don't jump when your lackeys give orders, Harlan." He and Mickey should have salted that letter before they burned it. Or sprinkled it with holy water. Maybe he ought to call the Ghost-busters to get rid of the haunting, ghastly Harlan Longfellow once and for all.

Roy didn't know if his grandfather took offense to his words or to his tone, or if his comment was what made him fall silent. He almost hung up again, except for a cough at the other end of the line. "Bill ordered you to my office? You didn't accept my offer to come see family in Boston?"

"Even if it had been an offer, I wouldn't be there. We're not family. Not after what you did to my mother. And since we're not family, and we don't do business together, I really don't see why you continue to sic your lawyer on me, Harlan. There's nothing we need to say to each other." Roy paused. "Well, there is one thing. Good-bye."

He turned off his ringer and lay down again. Closing his eyes didn't help. Neither did flipping over his pillow. With a sigh, Roy flipped back the covers. He was awake for the day now. Six hours wasn't enough, but he was too riled to fall back asleep.

He woke up more in the shower, then stumbled back to his room. He moved his worn jeans from the chair in the corner into the laundry basket and pulled a new pair from the wardrobe. After a glance at the temperature icon on his security system display, he pulled a thick sweater out of his closet. He was so seldom up this early that he had to mark the occasion the best way he knew how.

By the Cup was through its initial morning rush. Those heading to work had already picked up their morning beverages, and the high school crowd wasn't due for another twenty minutes, leaving Roy alone with his flat white. It was a rare treat, and he was determined to enjoy it fully.

The café was a small storefront on Lakeside Drive, with half a dozen bistro tables crowded into the space. A small glass case displayed the day's baked offerings, and a long wooden counter spanned the rest of the wall. The counter turned the corner to cover the short wall at the back of the room. It had second till at the other end to take care of the sandwich and hot breakfast orders prepared at the grill at the far end. It did good business in the mornings and early afternoons. Come summer, Lakeside Cones and Sundaes, the ice-cream parlor taking up the other half of the building, would pick up the same customers in the late afternoon and evening for a variety of cold treats.

Roy was debating a second cup, weighing the taste against the inevitable caffeine crash when he was entirely distracted by Lucy striding into the small coffee shop. She sidestepped the chipped tile at the front door, a move he knew well since he'd been doing it for years, before stepping to the counter and ordering three coffees but declining the barista's offer for a pastry.

"Hello," she said, stepping away from the counter until her order was ready. "I haven't run into you here before. Isn't this awfully early for you?"

"It is. No pastries today?"

Lucy shook her head. "Maybe tomorrow. Are you telling me you got up this early for a Danish?"

"It was a donut, but no. A phone call woke me. Harlan Longfellow decided this morning was the morning that he should insert himself into my life."

"Harlan Longfellow, your grandfather? The president and CEO of Longfellow Family hotel Harlan Longfellow? The man himself?" Lucy's blue eyes were comically wide.

"Yes. You sound impressed. Have you met him?"

"No. I don't know anybody who has. That's why I'm so shocked. I was half-convinced he was a figment of the board's imagination. He never deals with anybody below the executive suites."

"He deals with me. At seven in the morning. He was irked that when his lawyer said jump, I didn't ask how high." The thought the man expected immediate obedience annoyed Roy all over again.

"Did he say what he wanted from you?"

"I didn't give him the chance."

His annoyance grew when she flinched at his response. Lucy was in no position to judge him. "What? You don't approve? Do you think I should give him a chance after what he did to my mother?"

"No, that's not what I'm saying. I don't know anything about your family dynamics beyond the little you've told me. My response was based on years of occupational experience."

"What?"

"You're ignoring him and not dealing with the problems he's causing in your life. That is one hundred percent your choice and I'm not saying a word about it. It's also something I've learned not to do at work. If you ignore a problem in a building, it grows until it's out of control and you have to drop everything to deal with it, no matter what else may be happening at the time. That's how a leak under the sink turns into a new bathroom vanity, a week of mold removal, and replacing the ceiling in the bathroom on the floor under it." She grinned at him and, despite his mood, he had to grin back. She was obviously speaking from direct experience.

After a sip of her coffee, she continued. "Are you sure you don't want to deal with Harlan now so whatever he wants isn't hanging over your head?"

"Positive."

She nodded. "Okay. What are you going to do instead?"

"I'm going to ask a pretty lady on another date. Are you up for it?"

She smiled, then gave her head a small shake. "That sounds like a great alternative. What did you have in mind?"

CHAPTER 17

TWO DATES in a week was a new record for Lucy. Two dates in six months was too, with her work schedule, but when Roy asked her at breakfast if she was available for supper at six thirty the next night, she said yes. Now they were off on another adventure. Luckily, this time she didn't have to wear seven additional layers to ward off frostbite.

They pulled into a parking lot beside a three-story building. Lucy saw figures moving behind curtains on the second and third floors, but the main floor was a solid brick wall with no windows at all. "What is this place?"

"Come and find out." Roy helped her out of the truck and held her hand as they crossed the icy lot, which was nearly full. As they rounded the corner onto Richmond Road, she saw the building's storefront and sign. "Thunder Lanes?"

"I wanted to do something with you that gave us a chance to talk, rather than sit in a dark movie theater for two hours. What do you think? We can still make the show if you'd rather do that."

"I love it! I haven't been bowling in forever." It had to be a few years since she'd last strapped on rented bowling shoes. "You aren't a ringer, are you? Will I be playing against the league's top scorer for the last five years?" Not that she minded losing a fair game, but public humiliation was something else.

"No, I'm not part of the league. I can't remember the last time I bowled. This should be a fun and slightly painful experience for both of us."

"Then lead on."

The lobby had a large staircase off to one side, heading upstairs. A large set of apartment mailboxes took a portion of the wall. Opposite those was a set of glass double doors. The second they opened, the unmistakable sound of bowling balls landing on wood and crashing pins spilled out. "After you, Ms. Callahan."

She and Roy were assigned the lane at the end. The others filled up rapidly with teams wearing matching shirts and carrying ball bags. Roy excused himself for a minute, then came back smiling. "I didn't realize it was Seniors League night, but they only take up six lanes, so we should be fine."

"Great! We'll keep our low scores over here and try not to get discouraged by all the octogenarians congrat-ulating each other about their strikes," she joked. She stood and spun her arms in windmills to loosen up her muscles. Roy made fun of her, so she stuck her tongue out and proceeded to start deep squats with her arms stuck out in front of her. "At least I'll be able to walk tomorrow," she said in response to his teasing.

Roy got a strike his first time up, which set the mood for the night. Lucy tossed her first ball down the lane when all the lights in the alley flickered. "What was that?" she asked. "Is it too easy with the lights on? Are we playing in the dark?"

"I don't know," Roy said as they flickered again.

Then the sound system hissed to life, cutting off the golden oldies for an announcement. "Ladies and gentlemen, it's the first Monday of the month, so you know what that means," the voice coming through the speakers said. "It's time to glow bowl."

Pot lights scattered across the ceiling sprang to life as others went dark. All of a sudden, various parts of Lucy's outfit sprang to life, including the embroidered flowers on her leather belt and the cuffs of her jeans, as well as the pinstripes in her blouse. Roy got lucky. His shirt was blue and green, neither of which lit up. His white sports socks, however, lit up like glowsticks hiding in his pantlegs.

He stumbled over his feet when he took his next turn. "These things are distracting," he grumbled. "I think they're bright enough to throw their own shadows."

He wasn't wrong.

The automatic scoreboard was recording Lucy's split at the end of the fourth frame when she noticed they had company. Two people had slipped onto the bench across from the one she and Roy were using. The couple wore matching Hawaiian shirts: white palm trees and name crests burst off their flamingo pink backgrounds.

"Hello," Lucy said amiably, wondering if the pair knew they were horning in on a date.

"So, you're Roy's new girl, are you?" the man said. Both had heads full of powder white hair, but he towered a foot above his partner. "You look like the big city type."

"I am times two." If they'd seen her around town flashing her business cards, that impression would only be reinforced by tonight. Lucy knew she was over-dressed for a night of bowling. Without knowing where they were going, she'd put on a pair of dangly earrings and a bracelet with matching glass beads that caught the black light. Since glow bowling was already a thing, maybe she could invent glam bowling.

"Lucy, may I introduce Gene and Jean Wyatt, two of the four members of the Pin Heads, the seniors' bowling team sponsored by the Escape Room. Gene and Jean, this is Lucy Callahan. She's doing some upgrades at the Dew Drop Inn for the next week or two, and, yes, this is our second date. Now go back to your league and spread the news so we can get on with it," Roy said, shooing them away with his hands.

They refused to shoo. "Are you taking this lovely young lady out for dinner after your game?"

"Or dessert?" Jean added.

"Not tonight. I have an early start tomorrow. I have a date with a broken closet door track," Lucy said. She was two weeks into her stay, and she'd finished eight rooms and one suite to the point where she'd put the president in them if a White House entourage appeared in Holiday Beach. The rest of the rooms, though. She mentally shook her head at the thought. She needed two more weeks to bring them up to the same level.

"That's simply unacceptable. Roy Wagner, I insist you take Lucy out for dessert after you're done here. Everybody needs to end a date with something sweet. Of course, if she's against pie, a sweet kiss would do."

"Goodbye, Jean."

Lucy thought they were sweet, but the little old lady's words must have rattled Roy more than her, since he threw three gutter balls in a row. She wanted to tease him but decided it would be more effective when he drove her home. After they finished their game, she asked, "Is taking all this time off going to cause problems for you at work?" she asked.

"Surprisingly, no. Mickey is thrilled I'm actually using my vacation days. Apparently, my constant supervision is throttling his creativity. Since he hasn't managed to burn the place down yet, I'm going to keep letting him be my relief."

"What creativity is he talking about?" The two times she'd seen his brother, he'd faded into the background. Mickey hadn't displayed the same exuberant, extroverted personality as Emily or Roy.

"I don't know. That's the scary thing. But he's happy and Emily says he has it under control, so I'm going to suggest a second game since we have the time."

"Are you ready to go again?" She finished eleven points behind him and wanted a rematch.

"Prepare to get trounced. That was only my warm-up game."

Throughout the evening, more people stopped by to talk to Roy and, she assumed, check her out. It reminded her of a staff Christmas party where people from different departments introduced themselves to the newbie, only without the formality. Lucy didn't mind, although she did think it was a little strange since she wasn't staying in Holiday Beach. They all seemed friendly enough. Even more gratifying was Roy trying to get rid of them as quickly as possible so they could have the night to themselves.

"Tell me, Mr. Two Strikes in a Row, what's the next big event in Holiday Beach? St. Patrick's Day itself?" she asked. The bar had been advertising green beer and half-price wings on the seventeenth. One restaurant was offering a breakfast buffet offering green eggs and ham for the whole week preceding St. Patrick's Day.

"Do you mean aside from the Junior Shamrock Baking Championship on Wednesday? We have one more thing between now and then, but it's not specifically St. Patrick's Day related. The local hospital is having a fundraiser. A poker derby. They organize it with the snowmobile club and split the proceeds. It can be a little iffy at this time of year, but this is going to be a good one thanks to the cold weather keeping the snow around."

"I don't know what a poker derby is," Lucy said. Playing poker outside in March didn't sound like a good time.

"It's also called a poker run. Riders go to designated

locations and draw cards. Whoever has the best hand at the end of the run wins the pot," Roy explained. "The parking lot between the Escape Room and the Dew Drop Inn is usually one of the stops. It'll be a lot easier this year with those concrete dividers out of the way. The riders won't stay for long, but it would be nice if the volunteers could use the facilities. It's a long afternoon standing in the cold."

"Of course, they can come in to warm up. I'll talk to Brooke and Gloria and see if we can have an urn of coffee or something." Technically she needed the go-ahead from Gloria, even though she had more seniority with the company. She'd book the room and provide the hot beverages herself, but Lucy didn't think it would be necessary. Missives from head office had been coming out fast and furious for the last six months, telling all hotel properties to find low-cost ways to get good press within their communities. This event was made to order. Low cost—check. Community involvement—check. Fundraising for a hospital—double check.

"It's too bad you won't have a chance to get out there one more time."

"As a member of the club, I'm willing to make the sacrifice. There's always next winter. Besides, we had a good long run this year. I'm ready for spring."

"Me too." Although spring meant she'd be done in Holiday Beach. She'd be somewhere new with a new list of things to fix.

Roy nudged her when she didn't get up for her turn. Lucy sprang to her feet and hefted a heavy black ball. She took note of the weight in her hand. She needed to concentrate on the here and now and enjoy her assignment in this surprising small town, because she had a feeling her time with Roy in Holiday Beach was going to end far too soon.

CHAPTER 18

LUCY SPLURGED and bought a new blouse for her debut as a celebrity judge: green, of course. She hit the department store first but ended up finding the perfect top at Taylor Wear for Her, a ladies' wear boutique on Richmond Road that was just getting their summer collection in. It was an interesting shop, catering to both locals and the tourists they were expecting. It had lots of heavy camping clothes on one wall, and gauzy, bright beachwear on the other. Lucy found her blouse at the back of the store where the business wear was next to a rack of scrubs and uniform blouses and pants.

She also picked up a green tie at the attached men's shop. Since Roy hadn't stopped her from volunteering, she'd informed him he was going to be her escort and assistant for the evening. Mickey laughed himself silly when he heard, and he volunteered to come in for a couple hours on his night off just to make sure his brother was available. Roy tried to protest, but she said since he didn't have to eat anything, the least he could do was carry her antacids.

Lucy pulled her hair back with a thick black hairband and touched up her lip gloss before she left her room. Her ski jacket was clean and dry again. She hoped it would survive the night, but she wasn't going to bet on it. She refused to worry about it when she could spend all her time worrying about the culinary wonders she was about to encounter.

She met Roy in the parking lot of the Schultz Middle School. They joined the crowd filing in through the main doors and followed the flow to the gymnasium, which had been decorated with green streamers. Josh Huntington greeted them at the door. "Ms. Callahan, we're so glad you could make it. Our junior bakers are almost set up. Feel free to look around. We'll call you and the other judges to the stage when we're ready to begin."

Lucy counted twenty tables, each covered with a paper St. Patrick's Day tablecloth, decorated shamrocks, leprechauns, or pots of gold and rainbows. The children behind them were equally festooned, most of them with face paint of one of the same holiday symbols, except one little boy who'd gone for a completely green face. She saw cupcake carrying containers, two fancy cake stands, a waffle maker, and, to her confusion, a portable electric barbecue grill. She looked at Roy, hoping for an explanation, but he shrugged and moved her to the front of the room.

"Lucy, may I introduce my good friend Tripp

Turner. He and his wife Habibah own the Atlas Restaurant," Roy said.

"Oh, so we have a professional chef on the panel. Excellent. Pleased to meet you," she said. Tripp looked like a friendly fellow and he was obviously well known in the community judging by the number of people calling out hellos to him.

"Habibah should be the judge. She's the real genius in the kitchen. But there's bound to be bacon in some of these goodies and she doesn't eat pork so I'm here instead." He didn't manage to fully suppress his shiver. "I did it last year too. It was an experience."

"A good experience?"

"A   unique   experience.   Eye-opening. Unforgettable."

"Interesting word choices, Tripp. You aren't convincing me this is a good thing."

"Do it for the kiddies. We had these little contestants talking about it all year when they came into the restaurant. It means the world to the future little Anthony Bourdains and Giada de Laurentiises."

Josh strode to the center of the stage and raised his hands. "Ladies, gentlemen, contestants, and cheer squads. Please give me your attention while I introduce the judges for the fourth annual Junior St. Patrick's Day Baking Championship."

He called Tripp up first. It wasn't until she saw him take a firm grip on the handrail for the short staircase leading up to the stage that she realized he walked with a limp. Then a flip of his pantleg revealed a flash of metal.

"He lost his leg in an army accident," Roy said quietly, answering her unvoiced question.

Lucy nodded and returned her attention to the stage. Josh called up the second guest judge, Rachel Best, who Lucy recognized from her trips to By the Cup, although she hadn't realized the quiet brunette behind the counter was the owner.

Then it was her turn. "Our third judge is a visitor to Holiday Beach. Lucy Callahan works at the Dew Drop Inn and is visiting our town this month. Thank you in advance to all our judges. And now, let the tasting begin!"

Lucy expected chocolate chip cookies with the batter dyed green. Green cupcakes piled high with green frosting. Iced sugar cookies cut into shamrocks and doused with green sprinkles. She wasn't disappointed. But there were a few pleasant surprises.

She was certain the Guinness chocolate cake had to be a parent's suggestion, but when Lucy spoke to the young baker, the girl told her it was an old family recipe that her grandma got from a cousin in Ireland, and how she learned how to make it for her dad's birthday. The decadent, moist cake went to the top of her list of favorites.

The next contestant held up a platter of rolled, shaped cookies, with blinding green frosting. "I'm Dwayne Jackson. Would you like to try a shamrock cookie?" he asked.

"Wow," Lucy said, "you managed to get your dough really green. How did you do that?"

"They're gelatin cookies. I found the recipe in a cookbook, so I tried it. My mom said they were good."

"Jackson? Are you Glenna Jackson's son?" Rachel asked.

"Yes. She had to stay on the farm but my dad is with me here tonight."

"I saw him earlier," Tripp said. He bent over to take a closer look at the plate. "I remember these from when I was a kid. You used a package of Jell-O in them, right? It makes it really chewy. Did you use lime?"

"Uh-huh," the kid said, nodding vigorously. "I made lots of practice batches, but for the contest I put in two boxes so they'd be extra green."

Lucy heard Tripp gulp. "I'm sure they will be great. Judges, shall we give them a try?"

She let Tripp go first. He picked up the cookie, gave it a sniff and an approving nod. Then he nibbled the edge of the cookie. She heard his teeth snap together when the piece finally broke off.

Unsure as to what that meant, she took her own small bite. Or she tried to. Try as she might, she could not chew through the cookie. She held it in her hands and tried to snap off a piece, thinking it might be like crisp gingerbread, but it didn't budge. She tried another bite and eventually a crumb broke off.

The little boy looked up at her hopefully. "You can definitely taste the lime. And the cookie holds it shape really well," she said. Lucy paused there, trying to think of something else positive to say.

Fortunately, Rachel jumped in. "I like the way you

can still see the cookie cutter design in the cookie. Those specialty rolling pins can be tricky to use."

"I like extra lime flavor and chewiness," was Tripp's contribution.

They left the kid smiling, which is all they could ask for. The pound cake with green jujubes in it at the next table tasted wonderful by comparison, even if Lucy did need half a bottle of water to get the sugary taste out of her mouth.

"That was very diplomatic," Roy said as he held her bottle for her.

"My mom used to say there was always something positive you could say about another person's best try."

"She was a smart lady."

Lucy tried to hold on to that sentiment, because the next table, the one with the waffle maker, would have stumped even her mother.

The baker at the station hadn't been around on Lucy's first past. This time, she came across a familiar face standing anxiously on the sidelines. "You're Shelly. You had the runaway dog."

"Don't worry. Mom didn't let me bring him. She thought he'd be a distraction."

They had to wait while June Pham, Shelly's older sister, cooked the waffles fresh for them. Lucy was getting used to green batter, but this one looked like it had a different texture than the others. The young chef placed one on each plate, then spoke as she reached under the table for two covered containers.

"I mixed the batter at home and kept it chilled till it was time to cook them," June said. Her mother, standing behind the table, nodded. "I also prepared the whipped cream at home too, fresh. And I made the syrup myself on the stove."

"Those are quite the preparations," Tripp said. "I'm impressed."

"Did you use green food coloring in the batter?" Rachel asked.

"No. I was going to, but I used my mom's matcha tea instead."

"You did what?" June's mom asked.

"It's okay, Mom. I saw it on *Britain's Best Baker.*" She prized the lid off the first bowl. "This is my homemade kiwi syrup." There were bits of brown fuzz floating in it. She poured a generous amount on each waffle, making sure each and every square was filled. "This is real whipped cream."

"It smells kind of minty," Lucy said.

"Spearmint," the girl agreed. "I added it at the last minute because it's green."

This time it was Lucy's turn to gulp. "I'll bet this is going to be unforgettable."

It was everything Tripp warned her about and more. "The waffle is crisp to perfection," was Lucy's comment. Fortunately, it was true, and the others agreed with her.

"The matcha and kiwi combination is something I've never had before," Tripp added.

The little girl begged them to finish their waffles. "Sweetie, they have to save room to try the other bakers' entries," her mom insisted.

"Thank you," Lucy said to the mother for getting her out of another bite.

"No, thank you," the mom replied, and Lucy knew it was for not running from the gym screaming.

"What place in town serves the hottest, burn your mouth off wings?" Lucy quietly asked Tripp as they walked to the next aisle.

"Mercury's. Why?"

"Because we are all going there, my treat, after we're done," Lucy said. "I hope the next kid has some talent."

"And good sense," Rachel added. "Kiwi, matcha, and spearmint. My taste buds will never forgive me."

Their prayers were answered. A straight-edged cake, made in an angel food pan, stood tall on a plate, with a light green icing decoratively swirled on the top and sides. "You have very nice decorating skills," Lucy said.

"Thanks. This is a pistachio cake. Are any of you allergic to nuts?" the tall, retainer-wearing boy asked.

When no-one objected, he cut them each a slice of cake. The inside was tinted a light green, just like a pistachio nut. A few crumbs fell to the plate, but it held together well. Tripp pressed down with his fork. "Nice texture to the sponge," he commented, his voice strangely serious.

It was light and sweet, but not too sweet, with the faint taste of pistachio, enough to notice but not over-powering. "Delicious," Rachel said.

The next table had green blondies, followed by green meringues, which were an impressive feat for an eleven-year-old, and more green cupcakes, these ones with chocolate chips.

The judging was easy, although there was some discussion as to the order of the top two places. Eventually, the pistachio cake baker came in first and the Guinness chocolate cake baker came in second. A boy who made green candied cherry drops rolled in graham cracker crumbs came in third. Ribbons were distributed, photos were taken, and the judges were released with thanks.

When they were back in Roy's truck, Lucy stuck her tongue out at him. "La la la?" she asked.

"What?"

She pulled it in. "Is it green?" she asked, and then showed him again.

He laughed, which she took as a yes. "Please take me to Mercury's to meet the others. I need to taste something not green or full of sugar."

Mercury's was another new Holiday Beach experience. Unlike the Escape Room, where you knew exactly where you were from the second you walked through the front door, Mercury's could have been any bar across the country. But the beer was cold, the wings were spicy, and the table was private, so they could discuss the contestants. Despite some of the barely edible concoctions the entrants came up with, the talk was mostly positive. They all admired the guts it took for a preteen to stand up and show a homemade creation to the public, and then stand by and watch it be judged.

Roy offered to drive her home too, since he was

finishing the rest of his shift at the bar. "Do you want to stop at the pharmacy for antacids?" he asked.

"I have some back in my room. I'll be taking advantage of the mega-sized bottle." Her stomach churned at the recent addition of the spicy barbecue wings, but at least she'd gotten the taste of sugar and spearmint out of her mouth.

She leaned back into the seat and pulled her waistband away from her stomach. "This was fun. I know Holiday Beach goes all out for its holidays as part of its tourism plan, but is it always like this? You told me about the parades. What about the other big dates on the calendar?" St. Patrick's Day wasn't a big event if you excluded green beer and Irish ancestry from the equation, but the town found a unique way to mark it. She wondered if the other events were as memorable.

"Valentine's Day has a Sweetheart Auction. Not a bachelor or bachelorette auction," he clarified. "People offer up services and the proceeds are donated to a long-term family stay home outside the children's hospital in Minneapolis. St. Patrick's Day has the baking competition. Easter has the parade and the egg hunt. We have a huge firework display at the beach for Independence Day. Jackson Farms has a corn maze and haunted house for Hallowe'en between their apples and evergreen seasons. Christmas is surprisingly quiet.

"*Christmas* is your slowest time?" Lucy parroted in disbelief.

"For stuff the town organizes. All the local groups do their own things. School pageants, church choirs, carolers in the seniors' homes." He paused to take a breath. "Craft shows from the local artists, sleigh rides down Main Street and Lakeside Drive. I'm sure there's more."

"Stop!" How hokey was it that every single event Roy mentioned made her smile a little more? Her mother had always been one to decorate their little apartment for the holidays with the little cut outs that elementary school teachers used in their classrooms. Various places she'd visited had concentrated on one holiday or the other: Mardi Gras in New Orleans, the Thanksgiving Parade in New York City, St. Patrick's Day in Boston. But to have them all in one place made her heart happy. "Knowing that, Holiday Beach just moved to the number one spot on my retirement plans."

"It *is* in the name."

"Did the original settlers really name the town after the calendar?"

Roy laughed. "Not at all. William Holiday was one of the town founders. There's also a local copper mine named after him. He went bust a few years after it was discovered, but the town and mine names stuck. The whole town-wide holiday celebration event calendar didn't become official till about five years ago."

"What does the Escape Room do to participate?"

"We auction off one of our bartenders and a limited bar selection for a party at Valentine's Day, and we do something for adults for Hallowe'en." Roy shifted in his seat, which was when Lucy finally noticed they were parked.

"That sounds like fun."

"Maybe you'll be here in October and can try it out for yourself." He smiled at her hopefully.

She returned it. She had vacation time coming up. "Maybe." She wished she could be. More than anything.

CHAPTER 19

LUCY ASKED Gloria to call a meeting for the entire Dew Drop Inn staff, which meant they had to wait for Brooke to return from putting the floor polisher in the closet after cleaning the front lobby.

"What's up?" the blonde asked, a lock of sweaty hair stuck to her forehead. Lucy felt bad since she was the one making all the messes, like leaving drywall dust tracks down the hall and bits of plaster in the bathtubs. Brooke's workload had probably doubled since her arrival, but the friendly housekeeper said it gave her guaranteed hours, and someone to talk to while she did it.

"We have an opportunity to participate in a local charity event," Gloria said. "Per the notice in the staff room—"

"You mean your office?" Brooke interrupted.

"Yes. Per the recent notice from Head Office advising Longfellow Family Hotels properties to get active in the community, we have now joined the

Escape Room as the fourth stop for the Holiday Beach Poker Derby on Saturday," Gloria finished.

The hotel manager had sat in stunned silence after Lucy first proposed her idea. Surprisingly, her only real objection was to the short notice. Like Lucy, Gloria had never participated in a poker derby. As soon as Lucy explained what little work they had to do—access to bathrooms and a coffee station—Gloria was all for it.

"That is so cool! Jordan is going to be thrilled," Brooke exclaimed.

"What do you know about this thing?" Gloria demanded. Her brown cheeks flushed, and her eyes sparked. "Give me the details, quick. Lucy didn't have many. What's a poker derby? How many people are coming to our hotel?"

Brooke accepted a mug of coffee from Gloria's private machine, pushed her bangs out of her eyes, and settled against the filing cabinet for a good chat. "The annual snowmobile poker derby is a big deal. There will be about a hundred and sixty snowmobilers registered. The Holiday Beach Trails Association sets up a course that is fifty miles long, with five stops where the riders draw a card. The usual stops are the Jackson farm, the highway rest stop, and the Bonfire Beach Campground. The Escape Room is the fourth stop. The last one is at the finish line in town."

"A hundred and sixty snowmobiles? I didn't know there were that many in all of Holiday Beach," Gloria exclaimed.

"That's just the number of machines. The derby draws people from across the state. Some of them will have passengers, so we should expect about 200 people in the parking lot."

"Does Jordan have her own machine?" Lucy asked. Knowing how athletic Brooke's daughter was, she wouldn't be surprised.

"No, she's still too young. She'll be riding with Denny. We swapped weekends so she could do it with her dad. It's their thing."

"That's some heavy father-daughter bonding. Hanging out in the cold for two hours."

Brooke laughed. "It is. Denny and I may be divorced, but we've worked hard to keep things amiable for Jordan's sake. It helps that she's such a good kid. If they want to do this together, I will happily fill Jordan full of hot chocolate and send her out with her dad."

"Is that something we need to do?" Gloria asked. "Feed everybody hot chocolate?" She held her phone in her hand and a note application was visible on the screen.

"Not the riders. The volunteers will set up a tent in the parking lot," Brooke explained. "They'd probably appreciate a place to warm up, and access to the facilities. The whole derby takes about two hours from start to finish, so we should assume they'll be here for three. Putting a coffee urn or hot chocolate in the lobby and marking the public bathrooms on the main floor will be more than enough."

Gloria's shoulders dropped, and tension eased from her face. "That's it? We can do that. We can even swing some donuts or cookies for the volunteers too."

"Perfect," Brooke said approvingly.

"What about you, Lucy?"

She shrugged. "I'll be wherever you need me." She knew nothing about snowmobiles even after being on one, or derbies, but she could wash coffee cups and replace empty milk cartons. She still had her long johns if Gloria wanted her to be outside.

"No, I meant, will the lobby be ready? Your schedule said you'd be painting the baseboards and window trim on Saturday."

Lucy shook her head. The lobby needed more work than she'd originally noticed. The entire hotel suffered from that illusion. She'd made great strides on the rooms she'd worked on, but the more she looked, the more she found to fix. Not looking wasn't an option; too many people had already done that.

She hadn't said anything to the women she worked with, but Lucy had sent a detailed report back to head office; the Dew Drop Inn was on the brink. She could halt the building's decline but reversing it in the time she had was beyond her abilities. It needed a major overhaul, not quality but patchwork repairs. "I'll switch things around and slap up a first coat in the lobby tomorrow. That may be an all-day affair, but it'll look a little better for the people we'll have running in and out. I'll push the rest of it into next week. Samuel French is also coming over to install the new stained glass window tomorrow. We aren't sure how long that will take."

"He's done already?" Gloria said. "That will make a great backdrop for the derby."

Lucy was glad she finished that project. Not only

would the hotel's exterior look better for it, but it would also get the Chamber of Commerce off her back. She still had to deal with old, cracking pipes, leaking window seals, and peeling paint, but she'd take her wins where she could get them.

"I'll bring the donuts," she promised.

"Then we're done. Good meeting, everybody," Gloria said.

Lucy spent the rest of the afternoon scraping old paint from the window frames in the Ruby Suite. She mentally composed a memo advising head office that new ones would be more efficient and would save them money in the long term. "Why am I wasting my time?" she muttered aloud. "They haven't responded to my last four emails." Her department manager and the people in charge of the budgets told her no as often as they said yes, so she wasn't upset by negative replies. Being ignored entirely was a new experience. It didn't speak well for them taking her request for a permanent position seriously either.

Friday morning arrived with a text from the Starlight Gallery, notifying her Samuel would be arriving at nine. Lucy donned her long underwear and prepared for a cold morning in an attic that was open to the elements. She hadn't realized her long johns would be such a useful purchase.

She held the front door open as Samuel French wheeled in the wrapped window. Since the inn didn't have an elevator, it was a two-person job to carry the heavy crate to the second floor. It was so heavy, they had to lift it up one step at a time. The narrow staircase to the attic was even worse. By the time they hauled it across the dusty floor, Lucy begged for a water break.

"Now that we're here and the window is here, how about you finally let me see your masterpiece?" Lucy pleaded. Ever since her tour of Holiday Beach with Roy, she'd been dying to see the design Samuel had come up with. From flamingos to an intricate plate of spaghetti, every window had a different color palate and was unique to its business. She had no idea which elements of the Dew Drop Inn Samuel had used for inspiration. No matter what he picked, the size and prominence of the window meant it would be easily seen from the parking lot. But she wanted to see it first.

"How about you wait till it's in? I promise it'll be worth it."

"Fine," she huffed. "It's not like I can peek when I'm holding it anyway."

"It won't be much longer," Samuel said, swiping a handkerchief across his forehead. "We need to prize out the plywood, lift the window into place, and secure it. Then come the insulation foam and the exterior trim. Then comes the grand reveal."

Lucy swallowed hard when he mentioned the trim. Samuel laughed. "Don't panic. I have a cherry picker and a crew coming for the outside work. I won't ask you to hang off the third-floor ledge. I don't like to do it at the best of times, and it's a big part of my job."

"Thank goodness! I don't mind washing exterior windows on the twentieth floor when I'm standing safely on a balcony but standing on the outside ledge of a roof isn't the same." Lucy preferred to keep her feet on the ground. She didn't even like rollercoasters. "Do you have an assistant or someone at the gallery who you usually work with? Not that I mind."

The dark-haired artist shook his head. "Not since the last artist-in-residence gave back my engagement ring and told me she was moving to Sedona."

"Ouch." If she hadn't met Roy first, Samuel would have grabbed her attention. He was good looking, talented, and funny. He would have been a catch.

He grinned, obviously not upset about telling the story. "Right? Breaking an engagement is one thing. Leaving me for Sedona? Not Paris, not Florence, or even New York City. Cruel!"

"Well, you've got me to help this morning." They grunted and heaved and raised the huge frame level with the hole in the wall. Then, with one careful shove, they slipped it perfectly into place.

"Hold it steady! Hold it!" Lucy's fingers froze as she steadied the heavy frame while Samuel fastened it into place. Then he added more shims and screws and eventually told her she could move one hand. Finally, he began peeling away thick layers of brown paper.

"Are you sure I can let go? If this falls out..."

"If it can move after all of that, it deserves its freedom." He stepped back, and his jaw dropped. "Lucy, come here. You have to see this."

Lucy kept her gaze focused down as she joined him. It took her a moment to work up the nerve to look at the window. What she saw there was enough to make her catch her breath. "Samuel! It's perfect." Dust motes sparkled in the sun shining through the new opening, leading to a rainbow of colors scattered on the floor. She brought her eyes up to the source.

A four-poster double bed with a white frame and red linens was centered in the window on a background of flowers and evergreen trees. The words "Dew Drop Inn" were arched around the top of the circular art piece. "It's gorgeous. Beyond gorgeous," she breathed. It looked like a bed dropped in the middle of a peaceful forest meadow.

"Still mad that I didn't show you beforehand?" Samuel asked.

"Yes! I could have been bragging about this for days already. I could have put it on the website. Shouted about its awesomeness from the rooftop. Well, not the roof top. Maybe from the third rung of a stepladder," Lucy said, swatting his arm. "Come on. Let's see how it looks from the outside."

She spared a moment to make sure both of the bare bulbs in the attic were working and dust-free, so they'd illuminate the window from behind as much as possible. Unlike the slow trip up the stairs, she flew down them, barely pausing to grab her coat from behind the check-in desk before racing into the parking lot. She had to stand in the middle of it to get the best view of the window, but it was worth it.

It lost a few details at that distance, but she could still make out the bed and the words. Lucy wasn't certain the two bulbs in the attic would be enough to properly showcase it in the dark, so she made a note to check it after sunset. She'd call an electrician to put in a new light if she had to.

Samuel stood to her left. Suddenly an arm wrapped around her shoulder from the right and squeezed. The end of Roy's scarf tickled her chin as he tugged her close. "That looks incredible."

She turned her head and hit the wall of Roy's chest. She slipped her arm around his waist and squeezed back. "I know. I'm thrilled. I need to hire a photographer and get it onto the website tomorrow. With proper credit to the artist, of course."

"I'm just glad you liked it," Samuel said, grinning at the two of them.

"I love it. Just like I'm sure I'll love the shade you're doing for me since you can get back to work on it," Roy added.

Samuel snickered. "Yes, it's back on my worktable. Lucy, I'm going to take off for lunch, then come back with my crew to finish the installation. Thanks for your help this morning."

"No problem. It was more than worth all the heavy lifting."

Samuel left, but Lucy didn't move. She couldn't take her eyes off the window. "I would happily come to work every day just to look at that. Could you imagine having something so beautiful in your own home?" she asked.

"Samuel does do private commissions, but he prefers to work locally, so you'd need a place in Holiday Beach."

"The reasons to stay keep multiplying." When she finally tore her gaze from the hotel, she noticed a gigantic blue and white striped tent at the edge of the parking lot. "What is that?"

"The volunteer and check-in tent for the poker derby."

"I didn't expect it to be up a day early."

"Is it a problem?"

"No, just a surprise. Kind of like you. Why are you here so early?" In her head, she placed Roy in the same slot as a night manager, which meant mornings didn't exist for him. At best, he should be just rolling out of bed at lunchtime.

"I'm ready for breakfast, which I hope coincides with your lunch break. I have a hankering for a breakfast burrito, and Tripp will make me one at any hour, especially if I give him a chance to show off his soup and sandwich combination to another customer."

He'd gotten out of bed at the crack of noon just for her. Lucy's heart warmed even as her fingers froze. "Let me grab my purse."

CHAPTER 20

SATURDAY MORNING CAME EARLY. So early, Roy almost saw the literal dawn. He put on an extra layer of clothes, then threw another sweater in the passenger seat for later when he was working in the volunteer's tent, and headed out to fuel up for the event. He had just enough time for breakfast before the derby was scheduled to start.

It had taken a lot of convincing, but Lucy finally agreed to meet him at the American Table for green St. Patrick's Day pancakes before they changed the menu. He'd had to bribe her with picking up the bill and buying her a new toothbrush. She claimed her old one was worn out after the last batch of green-dyed food she'd eaten.

"Black coffee, your St. Patrick's Day small stack, and plain syrup, please," Lucy ordered.

Roy did the same, substituting a full order for the small stack and adding a side of bacon. "Is the Dew Drop Inn set up with everything you need?"

"I think so. We have a coffee urn in the lobby, and a kettle with hot chocolate packets beside it. Brooke has a mop and bucket on standby for all the snow and ice people will be tracking into the lobby. All we have left is picking up four flats of donuts after breakfast. Do you think that will be enough?" she asked, concern in her voice.

"Eight dozen donuts should be more than enough." At worst, she would have breakfast for a week.

"Do you wish you were riding in the derby rather than working at it?" Lucy asked as she carefully prodded her green pancakes.

He shrugged. He loved the feeling of flying across a snow-covered clearing, of launching his machine into the air off a snowbank and sinking into a soft drift on the landing. The cold, crisp air and the sun reflecting blindingly off the white landscape got his heart racing. But these days, so did other things. "It is a nice way to spend an afternoon. There's no prize for the first one to cross the finish line, so it's basically a couple hours with friends. But there's always next year."

When they returned to the hotel, a car interior heater hummed under the folding table set up at the back of the tent. Roy had a printed copy of all the registered teams and a pencil. "The cold will suck a computer's battery dead in under an hour," he said in explanation. Technology still hadn't caught up with a Minnesota winter.

The table also held three decks of cards.

"Wait a minute," Lucy protested. "How does that

work? If each deck only has fifty-two cards, and there are one hundred and sixty riders, we'll be short."

"Ha, ha, my good casino dealer, you forget. There are two jokers in every deck which makes one hundred and sixty-two cards, assuming we have no last-minute dropouts."

He saw the wheels turning in her head. "Yes," he said before she could ask, "a person could theoretically have a hand of five jokers. The record is two. We have had five of a kind more than once, though. Witnessing that is what's kept me from going to Vegas for a real gambling trip."

"Why?"

"Because it goes to show you the odds are never in your favor and anything is possible."

She shifted her chair closer. "That doesn't sound like a bad thing."

"It is when you're gambling with your own money."

"Fair enough." Lucy scooted over a little more, until the backs of their chairs touched. "I have a blanket. Do you want to share so we can conserve body heat while we wait for the first riders to arrive?"

They had at least forty minutes before that happened. "I thought you'd never ask."

Cuddling wasn't necessary. At first. The heater buzzing under the table took the edge off the cold, but the tent, with its canvas doors tied open, never reached warm. Lucy took a few minutes to run to the inn to fill two travel mugs full of cocoa. Unfortunately, her poor timing meant she missed the first snowmobile pull up.

Roy greeted the silver-haired couple by name. "Susan and Brian, you two are the first ones here."

"We have folks hot on our trail," the heavily bearded man said.

Lucy scurried back and set the mugs on the table. "I step away for a minute and leave you to handle everything by yourself. I'm sorry."

"It's fine. Lucy, let me introduce Susan and Brian Taylor. They run Taylor Wear for Him and Her. Brian and Susan, this is Lucy Callahan."

"We've already met," Susan said, waving a heavily mittened hand in greeting. "Lucy bought a blouse from the store. Did it suit the occasion like you'd hoped?"

"It was perfectly St. Patrick's Day appropriate," Lucy assured her. "I'm going to wear that color all year round now. I love it."

"That's great to hear."

Roy carefully marked them off the list, and then picked up a deck of cards. He tried to shuffle them without turning it into a game of 52 Card Pick-up. He'd like to blame his fumble-fingers on the cold, but the truth was he'd never learned to properly shuffle.

"For pity's sake, let me do that," Lucy begged after he picked up a dozen escaped cards for the second time. Before he could react, she scooped them out of his hands.

She cut the deck one-handed, then bridged the cards. With a bend to her wrist, cards from both piles flew into a single, perfect stack in the middle of the table. She grinned broadly when she realized she had an audience. "If you like that, get a load of this," Lucy said. She finished with a waterfall flourish, letting the cards stream from her raised right hand down to her left hand, which was still on the table.

"Are you a former blackjack dealer?" Brian asked.

"No. I just have a lot of evenings available for video tutorials about card tricks," she said.

Lucy fanned the cards, and Susan waved Brian forward. "It's your turn to pick."

He turned over the ten of spades. "Woo-hoo, four of a kind! Thanks, Lucy."

"All I did was shuffle."

"You did it very well!" Brian carefully stuck the card in the chest pocket of his snow suit and zipped it closed. "See you at the after party," he said as he and Susan returned to their snowmobile. He got on first, then Susan threw her leg over the back of the seat and snuggled up behind him. Brian started the machine with a roar, and they sped out of the parking lot, leaving a plume of flying snow in their wake.

The Mackenzie brothers were the next two snowmobiles to arrive. Mac whooped when he drew the ace of diamonds. Doug was equally pleased with his ten of hearts. "I'm one card away from a royal flush," he bragged.

"Go get your queen," Roy ordered.

He was certain he'd get to introduce the fourth rider to Lucy, but the weekday barista from By the Cup also knew the new girl in town. "Have you met everybody in Holiday Beach already?" he demanded during a lull. "You've only been here for three weeks."

"Maybe?" she hedged. "I keep forgetting how small

towns work. I've talked to more people here than I did in my last two jobs combined. Of course, at those jobs I was shopping at big box stores. Nobody remembers customers in those places."

"Well, you've certainly made an impression." A great one, by all accounts. "If you keep giving people the cards they want, they won't let you leave."

"All I do is shuffle. The rest is luck," she insisted.

Eventually, he did get to introduce her to the Jacksons who were participating in the derby. She waved to Dwayne, but she hadn't had a reason to meet the rest of the family who ran the specialty farm outside of town. She also hadn't met Mina Blackburn, who owned the Starlight Gallery where Sam had his shop, or the owner of the antique shop. Aaron Gillespie stopped by in his official capacity at the same time his teenaged son, Trevor, arrived on a snowmobile; they both took advantage of the warming station in the hotel.

One of the last teams to arrive was Jordan Portman and her father. The teenager dragged him to the table. "Dad, this is Lucy Callahan. She's working with mom right now, doing all kinds of repairs at the hotel. She knows how to plaster and fix plumbing and paint."

"Nice to meet you, Lucy. I hear you're also a superhero fan."

"I have to be. They're good for business. Somebody's got to do repairs after they're done beating up the bad guy," she teased back.

"Hi, Roy. We missed you at the poker game."

"I'll be back for the next one, Denny," he promised. He'd had to skip the last one because he'd been taking so much time off to spend with Lucy. She'd be gone soon enough, and he could get back to losing his chips to his friends. Despite their rocky start, Roy couldn't believe he'd gotten to the point where he'd rather spend time with Lucy than see the guys on a rare night off.

There were only three more snowmobiles after that. The moment he got a text confirming all the participants had crossed the finish line, he and Lucy raced for the inn. He downed a mug of hot coffee so quickly he didn't even taste it. He did feel a warm sensation melting the block of ice in his stomach as he sipped his second cup.

"That wasn't bad for my first time at a poker derby. Next time I'd like to participate though. I'd draw five completely useless cards, but it would be fun." She pulled off her toque, and it was all he could do not to laugh.

"Hat head, huh?" she said with a grimace, as she tried to fluff her matted hair.

"Little bit," he choked out.

"Thanks for asking me to sit with you. I had a good time. It was nice seeing everyone I've met outside of their businesses."

"No, thank you for keeping me company in the cold. This was the most fun I've had as a volunteer," Roy said. "I wish I could ask you out to dinner, but I have to work tonight." Mickey had been great about covering for him lately, but he didn't want to push his luck.

"It's okay. I plan to take a two-hour bath to shake this chill, and then then go to bed early," she said. He wasn't sure if she added the shiver for effect or if she was actually that cold.

Either way, he should let her get to it. "Can I text you later to see when we can go out again?"

She pulled out her phone and made a point of letting him see her turn the volume all the way up. "I'll be waiting."

CHAPTER 21

"THAT'S IT. I QUIT." Lucy threw her paintbrush in the concrete sink, tipped back her head, and growled at the ceiling. The stained ceiling, which she hadn't noticed before and now needed to add to her to-do list. She was loud enough to trigger a knock on the door.

"Lucy, are you okay in there?" Brooke asked from the hallway.

"No. I'm contemplating bloody murder."

There was a long pause. "Of anybody in the hotel?" Brooke asked carefully.

"No. Several people in Head Office in Boston better start watching their backs, though."

"That's fine. Can I come in and dump my mop bucket?"

"Sure. Just ignore the ranting maniac in the corner."

She deserved a good rant. She'd just checked her phone and wanted to toss it in the sink too. She'd filed a ton of reports in the last three weeks about the status of everything in the Dew Drop Inn, from the roof to the foundation. Her superiors back in Boston had instructed her to ignore half of them. Lucy wasn't happy, but the buck didn't stop with her.

Now she was getting emails from her supervisor's supervisors, two or three weeks after the fact, telling her to go ahead with the repairs. They had even flagged some of them as "urgent" and ordered her to stay an extra week if she needed to.

Which was good. In theory. The work needed to be done. But Lucy had already moved on to other tasks that needed doing, and there were more than enough to keep her busy. It was unheard of for her to spend a month at a property this small and she was just scratching the surface. After her initial requests were denied, she'd assumed she was supposed to make sure nothing fell down on guests' heads, and the rest of it would be dealt with in another round of repairs at a later date, with a full construction team instead of just her trying to do it all herself.

Even if she added a week to her stay, she'd be working ten- and twelve-hour days to do everything on her list. Two weeks would be better, but it would still be a never-ending to-do list. She had two-weeks scheduled over Easter as a vacation at the beginning of April and she wasn't prepared to give that up, so she had to be done in three weeks no matter what.

Her bad luck had struck again. Even worse, there hadn't been a word about her application for the new property maintenance manager position in the

Dallas/Fort Worth area. Not even confirmation they'd received it.

"Dare I ask why you're considering homicide?" Brooke asked.

Lucy took a breath and remembered to concentrate on one problem at a time. She'd stick to Minnesota at the moment. "Do you remember when I told you I wouldn't be replacing the carpet on the main stairwell? Or cutting out the worn flooring at the front door and retiling the entry?"

Brooke's brown eyes got bigger at each example. "Yes."

"Well, as of this afternoon, I'm doing both in the next two weeks. In addition to the rest of the repairs we've discussed."

A stunned silence hung between them.

"Why?"

"Because the folks in Longfellow Family Hotels' head office changed their minds."

"Are you doing it by yourself?"

"I hope not. It depends on whether or not I can get help."

"If you want..." The blonde's voice trailed off and she suddenly found her shoes very interesting.

Lucy sighed again. "Please don't let my foul mood rub off on you. What were you about to suggest?"

"Denny may know a carpeting guy. Do you want me to ask him?"

"That would be great. Feel free to give him my cell number if you think it would help."

Lucy took a few extra minutes to clean the sink, so

Brooke wouldn't be stuck doing it the next morning, before she escaped the inn without a coat. The clock above the bar that had 5s marking every hour was a welcome sight, as was Mickey's greeting of "It's five o'clock somewhere. What can I get you?"

"A large margarita, please. Be prepared for me to ask for a margarita chaser later." Lucy groaned as she sat on the barstool. It was still early enough in the afternoon that the bar was mostly empty, which was as much company as she could handle.

"Roy's talking with our distributor, but he'll be back soon," Mickey told her. He had the same brown eyes as his brother, and they were looking at her in concern. "Unless you want me to go and get him right now."

"Oh, no, I'm fine. I just got some news at work that's going to cause a lot of schedule shuffling." She didn't want to get into her troubles at the Dew Drop Inn in case Mickey had the same feelings toward the business as his brother.

"Did you know that was almost my mom's hotel? There was a family thing and my grandfather decided not to put her in charge of it, but she still always thought of it as hers. She and I used to have grand plans for that place," the young man said. He shovelled ice into the blender and measured the ingredients with swift precision. "Will you be tackling any specific projects?"

"The entrance. The old hardwood boards are coming out. I have to replace them."

"Please tell me you aren't replacing them with more boards. That entrance needs tile."

Lucy grinned for the first time that afternoon. "Exactly. Some large marble tiles. Maybe terrazzo. But not slate."

Mickey nodded enthusiastically. "Slate would get too slick with all the melted winter snow. Terrazzo would be great if you were repainting the lobby as well." He stared at her, waiting to see if she'd give anything away.

"Yes, we're repainting the lobby. And recarpeting the main staircase."

He pounded the bar. "I've wanted somebody to do that for years! You are so lucky. The Dew Drop Inn could be a jewel if the right people invested in it. You should see the place in the summer. The exterior and grounds need a major overhaul, but it could be a primo place for outdoor weddings. It would be booked solid all summer long."

That was more than she'd ever heard him speak. "Somebody like you is exactly what the Dew Drop needs. I'd offer you a job if I could. What's a visionary like you doing behind a bar?" His enthusiasm was infectious. Suddenly her to-do list seemed like more of a Hollywood hotel makeover scene instead of a monstrous pile of demolition and garbage.

He deflated at her comment. "It's the family business. It's mostly Roy's business, but I do have a degree in hospitality management. I could totally handle some place like the Dew Drop Inn."

She raised the glass to her lips. The lime, tequila, and sugar stung in the perfect combination of sour and sweet. "I'm not saying you're wasted as a bartender, because this is delicious. But as someone who has been stuck in a rut for far too long, I recommend you make the changes you want in your life sooner rather than later unless you don't want anything to change."

Mickey grinned at her. "Thanks for the advice."

Roy joined them after her second sip. "What are you two talking about so intensely?"

"Being stuck in a rut," Lucy said.

"The tables could use a wipe-down," Roy said to Mickey.

"Or you could just say you'll mind the bar while spending a few minutes with our lovely customer," Mickey said. "Thanks for the chat, Lucy."

"Anytime."

Roy watched his brother leave, but Lucy couldn't place the emotions behind his expression. Then he turned his attention back to her. "What rut?"

"I think I've been travelling too long. This assignment is wearing on me in a way that others haven't, which is odd because I'm really enjoying the town itself. It's just that even being in a suite can be claustrophobic. There's no place to go to get away from work when you live there," Lucy said. "I need a change."

"Are you looking seriously for something new?"

"More seriously by the day."

"Any luck?"

"No, as usual."

"Are you looking for a job in a big hotel in a city, or someplace small? Because Oliver Kowalski at the Fairlane Motel has been talking about retirement for the last two years. But that would require some management experience."

"I can handle a front desk if I have to, but that motel is outside the chain. I have my pension and seniority to think about."

"You mean because it's not a Longfellow Family hotel? This is true, but you haven't had any luck with them so far. Maybe it's time to expand your search parameters."

He took her empty glass and handed her a package of honey roasted peanuts. "You're in tough position. If you want my two cents, sometimes you need to shake things up. Take the leap and hope the net will appear. That's what I did when I switched this over to a beach bar with an escape room. The sports bar was doing okay, but I wanted more so I went out and got it."

He was right. If she wanted different results, she needed to make some changes. She wasn't about to walk away from her obligations in Holiday Beach, but what happened after that was up to her.

"That's good advice. Can I buy you a drink?"

Roy grabbed a glass and filled it with ginger ale. He raised it and waited for her to match his action. "You can only play it safe for so long. After that, you have to make a move, even if it's scary. Because it might be better than what you have, and even better than you dreamed," he said, his voice uncharacteristically serious. Serious, and seemingly directed at her lipstick, which thrilled her and scared her at the same time. "Here's for going after what you want," he said as a toast.

His look gave her courage, but she wasn't quite that brave yet. "And hoping it doesn't blow up in your face," said Lucy.

That broke the mood and made him laugh. "Was that necessary?"

"You've met me. You know my luck."

He'd only seen her get covered in green paint and get bowled over a by a dog. She had worse stories. But it must have been enough. "And hoping it doesn't blow up in your face," he echoed, clinking his glass to hers.

She smiled at him and the air was gone again.

"I'll drink to that," she said.

CHAPTER 22

HIS BROTHER WAS MISSING AGAIN. Which meant Roy had to cover the bar until he arrived again. Which was one more mark in the column of why he wouldn't be giving Mickey a raise. The kid—and behaviour like this showed he was still a kid because that's what he was acting like—needed to grow up and take the business seriously. It's not like they could afford to pay for time not worked during the winter season. They tended to run into the red as it was. The bar wouldn't be truly solvent until after the Memorial Day weekend, which was two months away.

He shouldn't have taken all that time off to be with Lucy. It had been a mistake to give Mickey all that freedom.

Although spending time with Lucy was not a mistake in any sense of the word. Roy had been wrong about her. Yes, she still worked for a horrible company, but she was a decent person. She was funny and kind and generous and gorgeous and...and he sounded like a lovestruck teenager.

But it had been a long time since he met someone who was such a good match. Once they started getting to know each other, they'd clicked immediately. The dating pool in Holiday Beach was pretty shallow, especially since he'd gone to school with a lot of the eligible women in town. Lucy was a breath of fresh air he didn't know he needed.

In fact, he could use her around right now to distract him from his growing frustration. How hard was it to show up on time? Roy had a list a mile long of things that needed to be done, from cleaning, to inventory, to figuring out a new payroll program. Mickey was a part-owner—as his baby brother so often reminded him; he should be taking some responsibility.

Roy heard the fountain hose hiss to life behind him. "Nice of you to finally show up. Be sure to mark your timesheet accordingly."

"I marked it when I came in. Three hours ago," was the cold reply he received.

"What?" He turned around and saw a very angry porcupine. Mickey stood as tall has he could, his hair sticked straight up, liberally streaked with sweat and dust. His black shirt was the same. But his scowl was what really caught Roy's attention. "What happened to you?"

"What do you mean 'what happened'? I've been doing the inventory you wanted done. It took a little longer than I thought so I'm ten minutes late getting behind the counter. I'll need another five to clean up, but I thought it might be worse than it looked so I asked Emily to stay a bit and she said she'd be willing to wait for me to finish."

"I sent her home. I've been covering for you." Mickey looked dirty enough to be have been moving boxes. "You did the entire inventory?" He tried to think of the last time Mickey had taken the initiative in anything and came up blank.

"Yes. Do you want to double-check it?"

"No, I believe you." His brother wouldn't be so defensive if he was bluffing. "I didn't realize that's where you were. I didn't know you'd been paying attention. You should have told me."

"I told Emily. And, as I said, I arranged for her to cover for me if I was a little late finishing." Mickey ran his hand through his hair. It didn't help. "I wish you'd give me the benefit of the doubt every once in a while, Roy. I do take this business seriously, even when you treat me like a joke."

Mickey gestured at the mostly empty bar. "We have about thirty minutes before the happy hour regulars arrive. Can you give me five minutes to clean up before you sign off on the inventory since you sent Emily home?"

"Sure, Mickey." Now he felt bad for assuming the worse. Cleaning the storage room was a terrible job, which was one of the reasons he so seldom did it. The job had been on his mind for weeks. Now he'd be good till they stocked up for Memorial Day weekend. It wouldn't even matter if Mickey did a poor job at it. The inventory was another issue entirely. He couldn't afford any mistakes with that.

It took Mikey seven minutes to reappear, but Roy was grateful to see he'd brought a fresh shirt to change into rather than just brushing off his old one. He almost said something about Mickey thinking ahead. Then he realized how condescending that comment would be. "Thanks for taking care of the storeroom. I know it takes a while. I really wasn't looking forward to it."

"I want you to see I'm pulling my weight around here," Mickey replied stiffly.

"I am seeing that." The door opened and a handful of patrons rolled in, clamoring for drinks before they'd even decided on a table. He couldn't leave Mickey alone when more were sure to follow. "I'll look at the inventory tomorrow."

"It may be a little off. I found that case of wine we couldn't find over Christmas. It got shoved behind the furnace, so I don't know if it's still good or if we now have twelve bottles of red wine vinegar, but it's in the back and well-marked."

Ouch. Roy remembered that case of wine. He'd asked Mickey if he'd taken it home for the family's Christmas dinner, and Mickey had said no. Roy assumed his brother hadn't wanted to pay for it out of pocket, so he'd written it off as an entertaining expense. That was two illusions shattered in a matter of minutes.

If Mickey kept it up for another month or two, he'd have to re-evaluate his raise.

CHAPTER 23

LUCY DABBED a little paint along the top of the window frame. "That should do it. How does it look?" she asked. She would have liked to do more: buy new furniture, swap out the three-paned window to a single big picture one. Still, a fresh coat of paint and new tiles at the entrance improved the room, bringing it up to a solid seven out of ten. She'd taken a chance; rather than painting all the walls a standard eggshell white, she'd painted one wall a deep burgundy that picked up some of the red from the wood trim in the lobby and up the staircase. It even picked up some of the highlights from the terrazzo tile she'd put at the front door.

"It looks great, but enough about work. Do you know where you're going for dinner?"

"We're going to the American Table. I've only been there for breakfast. Green pancakes don't seem like a fair sampling of the menu." She didn't care where they went. She'd been working hard and just wanted some conflict-free time outside the hotel talking about anything other than paint and plumbing repairs. Maybe they could get back to the same point they'd been at in the bar, where Roy had offered a toast and almost a kiss, and she'd panicked. Because she'd been practicing what to say in hopes—really strong hopes— that he'd make another overture. She'd been willing last time; this time she was ready.

But it didn't seem to be in the cards. It turned out Roy hadn't been having a great week either. "I don't begrudge Emily her vacation days. She's earned them, and it's better that she takes them now than over the summer, but it's leaving me in a jam. I may have to hire a part-time bartender for the week she's in Los Angeles." They were sharing a plate of the best potato skins Lucy had ever eaten, but all the bacon and melted cheese didn't seem to be cheering him up.

"Why can't Mickey cover for her? He's the assistant manager, isn't he?"

She thought it was an innocent question.

"On paper, maybe. But he's still a kid. I can't trust him with all that responsibility."

"I thought he's already been covering for you on the evenings you've taken off."

"He has."

"He mentioned that he was doing some inventory too."

"He did."

"Did he mess it up?"

"No, but it hasn't been busy either. If something

comes up, he doesn't have the experience to handle it. Managing is more than keeping an eye on the staff. It's payroll and scheduling and dealing with suppliers. He still has a lot to learn."

That didn't sound right. She'd only spoken with Mickey a couple times, but he seemed to know what he was doing. But this sounded more like family dynamics than a work problem. Either way, she wasn't going to stick her nose into Roy's business. "I'm sorry that's causing you so many problems."

"I'll deal with it. It's nice to see Emily so excited about her trip. I'm ninety-nine percent certain she expects to be discovered by a major talent agent at a nightclub or while she'd doing a tour of a movie studio. You should rub her head for luck before she leaves," he teased.

"It couldn't hurt. You'll be able to say you knew her before she got famous. Maybe she'll mention the bar in interviews. The Escape Room could host monthly Emily Jardine fan club meetings. You would have to name a drink after her, though. It's only fair."

Her distraction worked. They eventually decided it should be called the Em Tea Glass, and would be a variety of a Long Island Iced Tea. When Roy pulled up to the hotel, the gray cloud which had been hanging over them at the beginning of the evening was long gone.

"It looks like you're about to have a new guest," Roy said, indicating a gray sedan parked right next to the door.

"As long as they don't lean against any of the walls in the lobby, they're welcome." It was odd though, because Gloria hadn't mentioned anyone one with reservations who should be arriving that night.

She was hoping for a good night kiss, but when she turned back to Roy, she saw his attention was on a crowd of college-aged students stumbling out of the bar. Three of them rocked as they held on to each other for support. The fourth fell as he walked to a car.

"I've got to go," he said.

"Right. Bye." Lucy didn't know if he heard her. She barely had time to close the passenger door before he sped across the parking lot. "Thanks for a nice dinner," she said in the darkness. If she'd wanted him to kiss her the other night, the feeling had doubled since then. She was so tired of the one step forward, two steps back dance she was doing with Roy, when all she really wanted to do was step into his arms and let the rest of the world fade away for a minute. But he and the world didn't seem to be on board with that plan.

When she entered the lobby, the first thing she saw was a very frazzled Gloria speaking frantically to the man standing in front of the check-in counter. The manager wore a look of sheer panic. Lucy paused to see if Gloria was going to ask her to come over to help or wave her on because she had it under control.

"Here's another employee," Gloria said loudly. "Lucy, come over and say hello."

Lucy was grateful she was just coming off a date.

She looked more than presentable, and in tune with the upcoming holiday in her dressy green shirt and slacks. It made for a much better first impression than when she was in work clothes. "Hi, I'm Lucy Callahan."

"Harlan Longfellow," the stout man replied. He held out his hand. After the manicure, the first thing Lucy noticed was the substantial garnet pinky ring on his finger.

"Hello, Mr. Longfellow." She'd never seen the man in person before, even when she was in the head offices back in Boston. She half believed that all the photos of him in the company's promotional material were of a hired actor. Although now that she could see him in person, she saw some similarities between him and Roy. The same chin, the same eyes.

"Callahan. So you're the woman blowing the budget on this property." He didn't look impressed with her. It was hard to tell, though, because he'd been wearing the same grouchy expression when he'd been talking to Gloria. "Do you have any idea how much money you've spent in the last month?"

It was almost nine in the evening and she'd been enjoying her first night off in days. Until the last five minutes. "Yes, sir, I can tell you down to the penny, but not right now in the middle of the lobby."

"Lucy has been dealing with a backlog of repairs and renovations over the last month. She's doing a wonderful job of it with the added challenge of having to work around our guests," Gloria added. Lucy was grateful. This visit couldn't mean anything good.

They'd stand a better chance of getting through it if they covered each other's backs.

"We'll see about that. I'll be in the conference room at eight o'clock. I expect you and your receipts to be waiting for me," he instructed her. Then he turned away, and Lucy got the impression that she no longer existed to him. "I'll want to see you after lunch. Ms. Vargas. Have your assistant manager come in early to cover you."

"There is no assistant manager, Mr. Longfellow. The position has been open for almost two months. Lucy's been doing relief shifts since she got here to give me a break."

He let out a huff. "Then make sure she's available to cover the front desk while we're meeting. I'll make inquiries regarding the assistant manager position. Letting it go for over a month with a staff this size is unacceptable. Now tell me, which restaurants here deliver since there isn't an attached restaurant."

Lucy left the lobby at that point. Her brain and her temper were both going to explode. Aside from when she was on probation a decade earlier, she'd never had someone audit her expenses while she was in the middle of a job. She'd only been called in half a dozen times after the fact to have to justify some receipts, and every single time, management had decided in her favor. Having the company's owner and C.E.O. walk in and start questioning her judgment and profession-alism did nothing but set her on edge.

She was supposed to be basking in the afterglow of a lovely date with a handsome charming man. But he'd run off early, and now she'd be organizing receipts and invoices well into the night.

As she sat on her bed, surrounded by paper and with her laptop balanced precariously on her knees, Lucy made a disturbing discovery.

Tomorrow was Friday the thirteen.

She was doomed.

CHAPTER 24

SHE WAS NOT off to an auspicious start. Lucy choked on a dry muffin and washed it down with a swig of milk. Then she guzzled two cups of coffee to jump-start her brain. She would have liked to have a third, but any more would make her jittery, and she already had enough anxiety about her upcoming meeting.

At ten to eight, she tucked her laptop and envelope of invoices under her arm and headed to the conference room.

Harlan Longfellow was already there. From his half-drunk mug of coffee, he'd been there for a while. "You're late."

"I'm ten minutes early," Lucy countered. She bit her tongue immediately after the words escaped her mouth. She wasn't trying to be adversarial. She didn't want to start the meeting on the wrong foot.

"If you're not fifteen minutes early, you're late," Harlan insisted. "That's a rule among executives. But I guess I couldn't expect you to know that."

She managed to hold her tongue at that rebuke. She wanted to say the rule among contractors was a two-hour window after the stated arrival time, so she was more than early, but she knew it would do no good. They'd been in the room for thirty seconds and she'd already narrowed her outcomes to two choices: Harlan Longfellow was an unrepentant grump and nothing she could say would impress him, or he'd already made up his mind and she was about to be fired.

"I did my first property inspection on February sixteen. Where would you like to start—with my initial report, or would you rather do a room-by-room analysis?" Lucy asked.

"I have a copy of your initial report. I can't help but think you overestimated the amount of work that needed to be done. I assume you have photo documentation?" He raised a bushy eyebrow at her.

All of a sudden, the freezing cold afternoon she'd spent wandering around the outside of the inn was worthwhile. "Of course. Let me open my laptop and we'll start with the exterior."

Mr. Longfellow called a halt two hours after they started, and two minutes before she begged for a bathroom break for herself. She left the conference room and her shoulders slumped the moment she closed the door behind her.

"How's it going?" Gloria asked quietly from behind the registration desk.

Lucy just shook her head. Thorough wasn't the right word; brutally nitpicky was closer to the truth. The man questioned every decision she made. The only thing she hadn't had to answer for was replacing the cracked and broken windowpanes, and even that was close. When he questioned the line item, she called up the picture. She saw him open his mouth to comment, but she zoomed in one the photos before he had a chance to speak. When his lips pressed together, they moved on without another comment.

Yes, the stained glass window had been a necessity. The size of it had been her choice, so she was willing to take a little heat over it, but the stubborn old goat wouldn't even say it looked good. She thought it was worth every penny.

"If he asks, I'll be right back," she told Gloria. Then she headed outside. She didn't even return to her room to grab her coat. She needed to cool off.

The bar was dark and quiet. At least she didn't need to worry about Roy discovering his grandfather was in town. That was all she needed: to be accused of harboring his nemesis. She turned around to look at the inn, trying to think like a guest and not like an employee. After three weeks, what improvements would she see when she drove by?

The window in the attic was at the top of the list. It was warm and welcoming. All the windows were solid and they had matching shutters. The new paint job wasn't noticeable from the street, but as she walked into the building, it was what she didn't see that made an impression; no more peeling paint around the window frames.

Inside was a different story. The worn tiles were gone. A bright, stone floor reflected the lights from the new fixture above the front door. The lobby walls were a fresh cream rather than a dingy gray, and the accent wall looked stunning. She knew the carpeting on the staircase was due to be replaced, but she couldn't count on that now. It would be a huge improvement though.

She did not beat Mr. Longfellow back to the conference room, but she was within the fifteen-minute window he gave her. He checked his watch, sighed, and took his seat at the table. "Shall we move on to the suite repairs?" he asked.

"Of course."

Two more excruciating hours later, after Mr. Longfellow had scrutinized the last invoice and approved her remaining recommended repairs, Lucy escaped to her room near tears. The man was impossible. First, he'd questioned if her repairs were necessary, then he asked why she paid more that box store prices for material. She'd had to prove that a six-hour round trip to Minneapolis wouldn't be worth the savings once she factored in the time lost or the delivery fees.

And it was only noon.

When she finally found the energy to turn on her phone, she found seven texts waiting. Three were from contractors.

Four were from Roy.

An increasingly annoyed Roy.

Brooke says a H. Longfellow checked in. Is it him?

Never mind. Dumb question. He wouldn't come here.

Is it him? B talked to Gloria who said it was the owner.

Did you know? Is that why you're not responding?

This was all she needed. Lucy decided to bypass the back and forth and dialed Roy directly. Her luck held and it went directly to voicemail. "It's me," she began. "Yes, it's Harlan Longfellow himself. He was checking in when you dropped me off after supper. We had a discussion in the lobby, and I was up till midnight preparing for our meeting this morning. I've been in with him for the last four hours. Now I have to make up that work time this evening. I didn't hide anything. I didn't know he was coming. Will you call me when you get this?"

She explained, but she didn't apologize. She hadn't done anything to be sorry for.

The phone on the bedside table rang. "Hello?"

"Lucy, Mr. Longfellow is insisting on starting our meeting at one, which gives him time to get lunch and get back. Since you're supposed to cover the desk, I wanted to let you know you have to be done with lunch and back here in fifty minutes."

Lucy cursed. "Thirty-five. As a heads-up, I'm telling you now that if you aren't fifteen minutes early, he'll say you're late. Do better than I did."

"I'll be there. Does that leave enough time for you to get something to eat?"

It didn't. She could dash over to By the Cup and grab a premade sandwich, but that was it. "I'll be fine. Good luck with him."

Gloria's meeting only lasted two hours, but it must have been worse than hers, because Gloria came out in tears. She looked at Lucy, flinched, then dashed into the bathroom.

Mr. Longfellow showed no emotion as he approached the desk. "I understand the head house-keeper is Brooke Portman. I'll need to see her next."

"I don't know where she is at the moment."

"Find her. Ms. Vargas should be back at the desk. Where is she?"

"The bathroom. I'll find Brooke once she's back."

Lucy waited for him to return to the conference room before she scurried to the ladies' room. "Gloria, are you okay?"

"No. Why?"

"Because he wants to see Brooke now, and I don't think he's going to wait long."

"I'll be right out."

It took a couple minutes, but Gloria reappeared looking a little calmer. She still refused to look Lucy in the eye though. "I've got this. Brooke should be on the second floor."

Lucy's courage fled. She darted upstairs, told Brooke that Mr. Longfellow—yes, that Longfellow—wanted to see her in the conference room immediately. Then she stopped at her room, grabbed her jacket, and fled the building.

She ran into Roy in the parking lot. Literally. She was too busy looking over her shoulder to make sure the boogeyman wasn't chasing her that she wasn't watching where she was going. Roy's warm arm steadied her for a moment, then just as quickly let her go.

"It's good to see a friendly face," she said in greeting. Then she took another look at his face. It wasn't very friendly. "Or not. What's up?"

"I got your message."

"Talk about a shock. This is the first chance I've had to get away since last night." She wanted him to know she hadn't been avoiding him. She simply hadn't had time.

"What did you tell him?"

"About what?"

"Is that how you're going to play it?"

"Play what?"

"That's fine." Roy shrugged. "Longfellow Family Hotels strikes again."

"Strikes who?" she demanded. Everybody was blaming her for things today and she was getting tired of it.

"Are you really going to stand there and tell me you didn't know the C.E.O. was coming to the Dew Drop Inn? Why else would you have been working so hard to fix it up? I've told you what he's like."

"Thank you for noticing I've been busting my butt repairing the inn. I've been working that hard because it's my job. And I'll have you know I didn't have a clue he was going to show up, last night or at any time. I've never met Harlan Longfellow before last night. But right now, I sure can spot the family resemblance." The furrowed eyebrows and disappointed frown were identical between grandfather and grandson.

"That's not what I meant."

"I know. But I'm not going to stand here and let you insult me. I'm having a really terrible day. Gloria's is worse, and I still have to get to the store and get back to see if there's some way I can help for her before Mr. Longfellow calls another meeting. I don't know why you're mad at me, but I know why I'm annoyed at you. Goodbye, Roy."

By the Cup was busy. Lucy gave her order and was told to return in ten minutes to pick up her sandwich. She spent the time wandering the streets of Holiday Beach. If her time travelling the country with Longfellow Family Hotels was up, this charming Minnesota town might be a good place to land and start over. There was a lot to recommend it. Friendly folks— with one notable grumpy exception—in the cold of winter, with the potential of meeting more in the busy summer season. Decent restaurants and activities. When she was in urban withdrawal, a large city with all the amenities was only a three-hour drive away, to offer professional sports and four-story malls and an international airport. Roy would have been a strong reason to stay, but he wasn't the only one.

She returned to the coffee shop and found her hot sandwich on the counter, cooling. By the time she pulled into the parking lot, it was stone cold. She didn't care. It would still be the high point of her day.

CHAPTER 25

THE BAR WAS next to empty. Again. Roy hoped all the renovations Lucy had been doing would draw more folks to the hotel as word of the upgrades spread through the tourist community. He needed the business, badly. If the inn did better, the Escape Room did better. He could only imagine the sales he'd have if both places worked together like his parents had initially planned, but he could only work with what he had.

Every year, the six months between Thanksgiving and Memorial Day seemed to get worse. In the summer, he had triple the staff, and there was never an empty stool. In the winter, though, he was in competition with Mercury's and the bar in Bixby for a third of the clientele. If the hotel was fully booked all year round, he'd only benefit.

Tonight's lack of clientele meant he could handle the bar himself, since Mickey was in the office. The kid swore he was making progress on the new payroll program, but Roy would believe it when he saw it. He was already regretting buying the new app when the old one still did the job.

Over the years, he'd learned that change was rarely necessary. Revamping the bar once a decade kept things fresh and reinvigorated business. But swapping out computer programs that did the same thing, or upgrading a truck every two years because there was a new model? That was wasteful. Stick with what works: that was Roy's philosophy.

He heard movement behind him. "The old program worked just fine," he said to Mickey.

"The new one works even better. I figured it out. I've input everyone's hours for the week. I'll show you how to review them after we close, if you're interested."

"You figured it out?"

"They have a very responsive help desk," Mickey said. "Anyway, this new system will be much more efficient. You don't need to search for all the state taxes and deductions every time you use it. I've set and locked them. All we have to do is enter the person's hours and the program takes care of the rest."

"That sounds too easy."

"I'll show you. You'll love it. This will save us at least an hour a week. That's an extra-long lunch with Lucy as long as she's here," Mickey teased. His grin said he was happy for his big brother.

Roy didn't want to come down on him, not when he'd been working so hard, and was trying to support him. Mickey was thrilled that Roy had re-entered the dating pool after his latest dry spell. "I won't be having lunch with her anymore."

"Why not this time?"

"Because she didn't tell me that Harlan was in town. He's staying at the Dew Drop Inn."

"Harlan?"

"Our grandfather?"

"Is here?"

Roy wondered if he wore the same look when he'd heard the news. "He arrived last night. Lucy saw him. But she didn't tell me, then or today. I heard from Brooke in the parking lot. Lucy didn't say anything till I confronted her." She said she'd been busy, which was possible, but how could she think he wouldn't want to know about his grandfather?

"Is he coming over? Maybe I should go over there," Mickey said. The second comment sounded like it was made to himself.

"Why?"

"I want to see him."

"Again, why?"

Mickey got a look that Roy hadn't seen in years. It came from their father, who wore it when he was fighting to hold his temper. "That old man should know that our mother never gave up hope when it came to him. He should be told, to his face, that she would have welcomed him back at any time, even after the way he treated her, because he was family. Mom always said that knowing you'd be forgiven made it easier to make apologies."

Mickey had spent more time with their mother near the end than Roy had. Mickey had been attending college part-time while she was home sick, and Roy had been working at the bar. He'd been grateful that his little brother could keep an eye on her and keep her company. He'd known they'd talked, but he was shocked to hear that Harlan was one of their topics of conversation. But all their talking didn't change the truth.

"Harlan Longfellow isn't here to apologize. He doesn't care. He didn't come to see her when we were born. He didn't come to see us after Mom died. I don't think he's ever heard of the word "forgiveness." I don't know why he's in Holiday Beach, but it has nothing to do with family," Roy insisted.

"Probably not, but I think we should find out why he's in town," Mickey insisted.

"If you want to know so badly, you can go ask him. On your break," Roy stressed.

It turned out Mickey didn't have to make the trip across the parking lot. Just before nine o'clock, the door opened, and a stranger walked in. But this stranger he recognized.

A well-dressed, slow moving man unbuttoned his coat and unwound the scarf from his throat. He made his way to the bar, and put his coat, scarf, and hat on the stool beside him.

"Welcome to the Escape Room," Roy said, offering none of his normal warmth in the greeting. "What can I get you?" This close up, Roy could see his own face in the old man's features. Brown eyes, fully gray head of hair, deep wrinkles under his unnatural tan. At least Roy's was real.

The old man studied the bottles on the top shelf behind the bar. "Do you have any Guinness?"

"This close to St. Patrick's Day? The keg is still half full. A pint?"

"Please."

The thick brown liquid flowed slowly, and a generous head of foam topped the glass.

"Thank you. This is a nice place you have here. I assume it's yours?"

"Mine and my brother's. We're second-generation bar owners," Roy said proudly. "This place is one of Holiday Beach's oldest businesses. We're almost fifty years old."

The old man didn't touch his glass. Instead, he studied the room, focusing on the empty tables. "You aren't very busy for a Friday night."

"It'll pick up," Roy said flatly. "I hardly expected to see you here, Harlan."

"So you know who I am." The old man nodded in approval. Like Roy needed it. "Would it kill you to call me "Grandfather," Royal?"

"It's just Roy."

"I'm surprised your mother let you get away with that. She did love those Little House books. Your brother is lucky he wasn't named Almanzo."

It seems Harlan hadn't kept up with his grandsons, although Roy wasn't surprised. If he'd had the slightest bit of contact, he would have known Mickey's middle name was Charles, also from the popular series of children's books. "What do you want, old man?"

His grandfather had an impressive stare, but Roy refused to flinch. "I'm here to talk to my grandsons, to discuss the future of the Dew Drop Inn. I sent you a personal invitation to come to Boston to discuss this with me, but you couldn't be bothered to show up for the appointment. I had to fly halfway across the country with the intention of extending this olive branch. Now, after meeting you, I think I've wasted my time."

Roy took a step back from the bar top. Mostly so he didn't accidently reach across it and throttle the old man with his bare hands. "There are too many things wrong with that last statement to count, but I'm going to try. You didn't invite us to Boston. We received a registered letter from the law offices of William R. Truman the Third. Secondly, it wasn't an invitation. It was an order to appear. Third, no response is a response. It's a no. Besides, why would I want to come to Boston?"

"I'm your grandfather."

"Since when?" Roy shouted. Tiny and his buddies in the corner looked up, but Roy didn't care that he'd raised his voice. From the corner of his eye, he saw Mickey head in their direction. "It wasn't when I was born, and you didn't contact your daughter. Or when Mickey was. Or when you were absent for the next twenty years. Or when Mom died. At what point did you become our grandfather in any way beyond genetics?"

The man's complexion went from unnaturally brown to unnaturally red.

Roy pressed on. "I repeat, what do you want, Harlan?"

"I wasn't the father or the grandfather I should have been. I'm here to talk about how we can keep the Dew Drop Inn in the family. I'm getting older and it's time I buried the hatchet with my grandsons."

It was like Roy had entered the Twilight Zone. Or maybe Harlan had and thought his actions made sense. "You're right. The Dew Drop Inn should have always been in the family," Roy said. "When I was little, I heard my mom and dad talking about what our future would have been if it had been theirs. When my mom was in the hospital, she and Mickey talked about how they would have run it alongside the Escape Room to make it a little family partnership. But none of that happened because you decided you didn't want Larry Wagner to marry your daughter. It didn't happen then, so why are you so concerned about it happening now?" Suddenly, Mickey's offhand comment when they shredded the letter popped into his head. "Oh my God, you *are* dying."

"I'm eighty-five years old. Of course, I'm dying. Not imminently, but I want to get this one thing off my plate while I've still got all my marbles."

"This one thing being..."

"Doing what my stubborn, headstrong daughter refused to do!"

Roy officially lost all patience. The phone calls from the lawyer had been irritating; the letters, annoying. He could deal with upsetting Harlan Longfellow. But nobody insulted his mother. "She refused to give up the man she loved and the future they planned because you wanted a merger to form a hotel empire! I'm glad she refused. Mickey and I wouldn't be here otherwise. I think she made the better choice."

"No. That's not—"

"Get out of my bar, old man. I said it to your lawyer and now I'm saying it to you. We have no business to discuss. Now or ever. You have five minutes to get out of here before I have you arrested for trespassing."

Harlan struggled into his coat and pulled his hat tightly onto his head. "You are just like your mother."

"I've never had a better compliment from anyone in my life."

Mickey strolled back to the bar. He kept sneaking glances at Roy as he drew a fresh round of beers. Roy let him look. "Well?" Mickey finally asked.

"Well what?"

"What did he want? That was him, right?"

That's when Roy realized for all Harlan's talk about making amends with his family, he hadn't even asked to talk to his younger grandson. "Nothing."

"He didn't fly in from Boston and come to the bar for no reason at all. What did he say, Roy?"

"It's fine, kid."

"I'm not a kid, Roy. I haven't been for a long time. If it has to do with our family, it involves me. If it involves the bar, it involves me. If it involves you, it involves me. What did the great Harlan Longfellow want?"

"He said he's in Holiday Beach because we never

followed up on his invitation to come to Boston. He says he wants to try to heal the breach in the family, starting with giving us the Dew Drop Inn."

Mickey's dropped jaw said it all.

"I know."

"He wants to give us the hotel? Was he serious?"

"That's what he said. I told him to take a hike."

"Why?"

Roy shrugged. "Who knows why he's doing it now. He says he's not dying, but I don't know if we can trust him."

"Not him. You. Why would you turn down the hotel? You should have taken it and run."

"We don't want anything from that man."

"We want the hotel!" Mickey protested. "Are you kidding me? That's all Mom wanted for us."

"I don't think she'd want it if it came with Harlan."

Mickey threw up his hands. "We just had this conversation. She wouldn't have blinked before she said yes to that deal."

"We don't need it. We have the bar. Besides, what do we know about running a hotel?"

"Only two years of courses and a degree's worth, Roy. What do you think I studied at college?"

"You took bartending and some accounting classes."

"I took a whole hospitality degree, Roy. Including hotel, restaurant and bar management. Thanks for noticing."

"You can't think that you're ready to run a hotel.

You may have taken some classes, but you don't have the first idea of how it would work in the real world."

"I did a double practicum at the Fairmont Minneapolis for two months, working the night shift on the front desk and helping the assistant manager schedule over sixty people in five departments so I could get the experience you're talking about. When Lucy and I discussed the hotel, she said I had great ideas and would be an asset to any place lucky enough to take me."

"You spoke to Lucy about working at the Dew Drop Inn? How did she know you studied hotel management?" He knew she was a liar. She'd probably come to town to soften them up for her boss.

"Unlike you, she asked me what I studied at college. I could run a hotel. I could run this place too. I guess I should be grateful you promoted me to assistant manager, even if you won't let me do anything with the title."

"You can barely show up on time for work here," Roy protested.

"I'm here on time every day. You just haven't noticed."

"Then why aren't you at the bar when your shifts start?"

"Because I'm cleaning the storeroom. Or I'm fixing the damaged loading doors. Or learning the payroll system or rearranging the schedule when someone calls in sick or tracking down deliveries, so you don't freak out when they're late." He glanced over his shoulder and saw their few customers were still at their table and out of earshot. "I know the bar's been struggling, Roy. I've been doing everything I can to take some of the stress off your plate, even though you keep insisting everything is fine. You just haven't noticed. You've had people trying to help you for a while, but you can't see it. Don't you know what getting the hotel would mean to us, even taking Harlan out of the equation?"

"The Dew Drop Inn is a mess."

"I know you're upset but take a step back and look at the big picture. Lucy's worked wonders while she's been here. Can you imagine what we could do with a partnership between the businesses? If they got licenced for weddings or private parties, we'd be the supplier. This could be the exact break the bar needs. And you're going to throw it away because you're being as stubborn as Harlan is."

A red haze dropped over Roy's eyes. "That's not fair."

"The truth hurts, big brother. But it's not just hurting you this time. If you don't learn to forgive, you're going to lose everything that matters to you."

Mickey didn't wait for him to respond. He loaded a tray with the foaming glasses of beer, and left Roy standing alone behind the bar.

They weren't going to lose the bar. Having Harlan hand them the Dew Drop Inn on a silver platter wouldn't fix anything. He could make it work on his own, if only he could convince Mickey to help a little more instead of mooning over the property next door. But it seemed that might be too much to ask.

Lucy had mentioned Harlan said he'd come to town to review her work. She'd been right. She did have the worst luck of anyone he'd ever met, dragging Harlan to Holiday Beach with her. Only when it came to Roy, her bad luck rubbed off instead of the good.

CHAPTER 26

LUCY WAS on her way to her room with a still hot pizza box. She rounded the corner and saw Gloria behind the desk, unable to escape Harlan Longfellow's rant. Thankfully, the manager's shrug let her know Gloria wasn't the subject of the rant itself. She was just stuck in the general vicinity.

"That boy is just like his mother. There is nothing of me in him. Do you see any resemblance between me and my grandson, Ms. Vargas?"

"Sir, I don't know who your grandson is." She looked at Lucy.

"Roy Wagner next door," Lucy mouthed.

"Roy Wagner is your grandson?" Gloria exclaimed. The comment was aimed at Lucy, but unfortunately for her, she caught Harlan's attention.

"Do you know who my grandson is, Ms. Callahan?"

"Yes, I know Roy."

"Did you know of our relationship before I arrived?"

"Yes."

"Why didn't you say anything?"

"Because it wasn't relevant to how I did my job, Mr. Longfellow. When you didn't bring it up, I though you didn't want it mentioned at all." In fact, she'd prefer if nobody mentioned Roy to her at all for a few days, at least until the sting of his accusation faded.

"It's relevant because I arranged for you to come to the Dew Drop Inn specifically to dust the old place off so when I gave it to them, they'd be ready to hit the ground running. Is this place ready for a grand reopening under new management, Ms. Callahan?"

Lucy took a breath. She did not want to give that answer. Lying about it wouldn't do her any good either; the man had seen exactly what still needed to be done. "No, sir. Not for another two weeks at least." She'd slapped a little mascara and lipstick onto the old building. Two more weeks would give her time to make sure her repairs would last for a while.

"Well, you do that. Make this place look as good as you can. I want every dollar possible taken into account for the appraisal."

"Appraisal?"

"If I can't give this place away, I'm going to sell it. It's been an albatross for years. Now it's time to let it go."

"What do you mean "let it go"? Are you talking about selling the Dew Drop Inn?"

He stared at her. "I flew halfway across the country

to get rid of this place one way or another. If my grand-sons don't want it, somebody else will."

Gloria's hand was at her throat. Lucy heard Brooke gasp from around the corner. "What about your employees here?"

His response was as cold as the air outside. "They'll be able to submit applications to the new owners just like anybody else."

"Won't you transfer them to another property?"

"Not with their performance reviews." He looked to Gloria. "Please don't sniffle at the front desk."

He walked out the front door. Despite her deepest wishes, Lucy was certain it wasn't for good. "I don't believe it," she whispered.

Gloria was fighting hard not to break down. She wiped a tear away with her fist. Brooke appeared from around the corner. She didn't pretend to be unaffected by the devastating news. "At least you're safe. Did you know, or was that all a show?" Brooke asked.

"Know what?"

"That the hotel was changing ownership, one way or another. Did you know you were coming here to get it ready for sale?" the housekeeper demanded. "This place has been neglected for years. You show up to make it pretty, and a couple weeks later it goes on the market."

"She didn't set us up, Brooke," Gloria said.

It was kind of Gloria to defend her, but Lucy didn't need to drive another wedge between the coworkers. "I'm sorry. I really didn't know," Lucy said helplessly.

Brooke paused long enough to glare at her. "Of course, you didn't." Then she was gone.

"I guess I should update my resumé," Gloria said. "It looks better to submit an application when you're still employed." She sighed heavily. "I am not moving back to San Antonio. I don't care if I end up in Alaska. If I go home, my family will never let me out of their sights again."

"I've been to Alaska. It's a lifestyle, not just a place. If you're willing to travel, I can put out some feelers for you," Lucy offered. "But Brooke. With her daughter in school..."

Gloria shook her head in commiseration. "Yeah."

There was nothing left to say. When Lucy got back to her room, she put her entire pizza into the fridge. She'd lost her appetite. Which was better than her new friends losing their jobs. She threw herself facedown on her bed.

Friday the Thirteenth indeed. And there were still six hours to go.

CHAPTER 27

NOW THAT FRIDAY the Thirteen was over, Roy was determined to make Saturday the Fourteen a fresh start. The bar had the big St. Patrick's Day party coming up, and neither his argument with Mickey nor the visit from Harlan was going to spoil their biggest night of the spring.

He'd already picked up green food dye from the grocery store. Now he was off to Handler Hardware to pick up some lightbulbs. Colored bulbs got a surprising workout in his bar, and he'd dropped two green ones when he was swapping out the Christmas red and green for New Year's Eve yellow and blue.

Handler Hardware was doing brisk business on a Saturday morning. With spring on the horizon, people were beginning to plan ahead. Roy saw more than one basket filled with vegetable seeds and compostable seedling trays.

He also saw Lucy waiting in line, with a six-foot gap between her and the customer behind her. Then he watched Jordan Portman lead her dad down one aisle and up another to avoid getting close to her. He winced in sympathy at the hurt look on Lucy's face when she saw it, but he steeled his expression back to neutral before she saw him.

He was a person away when Lucy stepped to the counter. She unpacked her caulking and turpentine quietly. Julie hesitated before she rang it up. Then he heard Lucy ask, "Would you prefer if I bought my supplies online?"

Julie looked at her in surprise.

Roy pushed past the next person in line. "Seriously? Are you really threatening to take your business out of Holiday Beach?"

"No, you big jerk. I'm obviously making Julie's customers uncomfortable by being in her store, and she doesn't look overly pleased to see me either. I'm offering to leave so I don't cause more trouble," Lucy whispered harshly.

"No, Lucy, you don't have to leave," Julie quickly said. She began running items over the bar code scanner. "I just heard the news about the Dew Drop Inn and was really surprised." She bagged them and Lucy quickly paid with her credit card. Rather than get close to him, she skirted around the far side of the garden seed display and left.

When it was Roy's turn, he made sure he had Julie's attention when he said, "If she makes you uncomfortable, you can refuse service."

"No. Lucy's not the one selling the hotel. I shouldn't punish her for it. I was just surprised to hear it. Besides, she's given me a lot of extra business over the last month. I'm going to get every dollar from the hotel while I can."

He grudgingly conceded the point. Lucy had been good to the town while she was there. She'd also given a substantial bump to a lot of local contractors who were in a slow time before the summer people called them in for repairs to their cottages after the winter had its way with them.

Sam French had good news for him when he stopped at the Starlight Gallery. The store was empty, but Sam and Mina Blackburn were huddled around her laptop. Over their shoulders, Roy saw a series of graphs flashing on the screen. "What's so interesting?" he asked.

Mina spun the laptop to show him a rising trend. "See this? Those are hits on our website going through the roof. Our traffic has quadrupled in the last two days and we just figured out why," she gloated. Her purple eyes gleamed as she delivered her news.

Roy smiled and took the bait. "Why?"

"Because Sam's new window at the Dew Drop Inn got picked up by Darlene Howard. She's a very influential interior designer out of Chicago. She posted it on Instagram. He's sold two pieces in the last two days."

"I'm also in negotiations for two more commissions. You're lucky you got yours in early," Sam added. "Do you want to see it?"

"Absolutely."

The pool table light shade was everything he hoped for. The long side panels showed an assortment of pool cues and balls. The end pieces were colorful mosaics. "It's perfect. When can I take it home?" he asked.

"Pick a day, and I'll come over and help you hang it before you open," Sam offered. "I'd love to do another one sometime, but I think you were right to take out the third pool table and put in the Escape Room. What are you plans for it over the summer?"

"The events schedule is Mickey's baby. I'm sure he has something up his sleeve." It was the appropriate thing to say, but Roy didn't know if his brother did have any plans in the works. To be fair, he hadn't asked.

He didn't get a chance to when he showed up to handle the week's delivery. Mickey had already begun unloading the truck when Roy called a halt to the activity. "What is this?" he demanded. "I didn't order these extra cases of beer. And what's with all the rum? Mickey, what did you do?"

"I added an extra order for the party on Tuesday."

"I didn't authorize that. What were you thinking?" They had no need for all the extra beer and liquor waiting for homes in the storage room.

Mickey pulled out his phone. "Last year, we ran short on both Coors and Budweiser. I made a note of it after you had a fit about having to sell Corona at the same price." He referenced his screen and threw a bunch of numbers at Roy, citing cases purchased and how much they were short. He even listed it by brand. "As for the rum, the distributor was offering discounts this month. It's our brand, and we'll go through it eventually. If we cut our order next month, we'll still be ahead on the books without running short."

"How do you know all this. You weren't even assistant manager at this time last year."

"I knew I would be, so I paid attention. Is there anything else you want to talk about, or should I get back to work?" Mickey didn't even sound mad. He was just businesslike.

Roy didn't like it. It made him feel like he'd fallen down on the job somehow. "No, that's fine. I'll go swap out these lightbulbs."

"The ladder's leaning against the pool table. I set it out for you."

"Thanks." He didn't turn on the bar's sound system as he went around preparing for opening time. He preferred to stew in silence. It was hard coming to term with the fact Mickey had been covering his back for months and he hadn't noticed at all. He hadn't been giving his little brother nearly enough credit.

The fall from the pedestal of I'm the Boss and the Only One Doing Real Work Around Here left his ego a little bruised. The statue of My Baby Brother Isn't a Baby Anymore falling off the neighboring shelf and landing on his head didn't help.

When had everything turned upside down in his world?

Emily had the answer. She arrived just before they opened and asked, "Have you heard about what's going on next door? From the sound of it, Lucy's luck is at it again."

CHAPTER 28

THE DIAMOND SUITE was as perfect as the gem it was named after. There wasn't a single thing Lucy could do to make it any better than it already was. Her arms ached after spending the day putting up new wallpaper, but it was worth it. The Dew Drop Inn now had a magnificent signature suite.

It almost had two. All she had to do was finish scraping paint from the windows of the Sapphire Suite, and it would be ready for royalty as well. It hadn't been easy hanging the closet door on her own, but Lucy didn't feel right asking Brooke to hold it for her. The other woman had burst into tears the last time she'd seen Lucy's face, so Lucy found a way to do the job on her own.

Her own Emerald Suite needed a fresh coat of paint, and new bathroom lighting fixtures. Those were currently sitting in a box in her closet. Lucy planned to move to another room for two days to do the painting. After that, all she had left was the Ruby

Suite, but she couldn't get in there until Harlan Longfellow left. Overall, she was proud of what she'd done.

In all, she'd completely repaired and refreshed two of the suites and fourteen of the twenty rooms, and half the suites. The entire lobby was brand new, with the exception of the furniture. The exterior was as good as she could make it during the end of a Minnesota winter; the next people would have to finish the job in the summer. The attic's new picture window was stunning. She'd even managed to upgrade the laundry room.

Lucy figured she had another week to do as much as she could. She probably would not get to Gloria's office, or the boardroom. But if she could get the other two suites completely finished, and the last of the standard rooms up to at least a "B" grade, she'd count her time in Holiday Beach as a win.

Professionally.

She'd already informed her boss back in Boston that she was done after this job. She claimed exhaustion. She had oodles of vacation time saved and had already booked two weeks to enjoy her tiny apartment. She'd spend it eating fresh crab cakes sprinkled with Old Bay and reflecting on whether she wanted to continue down her current path or brave a new one. Lucy had been feeling hollow for a while. If she didn't stop now to refill her soul, she'd be permanently burned out by the end of the year.

"A whole fridge full of fresh food and a real oven to cook it in." She said the words out loud. She could access spas and room service whenever she wanted. She knew what true luxury was.

Lucy glanced at her mini-fridge and microwave and grimaced. She couldn't take another pizza. She was trying to remember if she had a frozen meal in the tiny freezer when her cell phone rang. She was surprized to see Brooke's name on the display.

"Hello? Brooke?"

No words came over the phone. Lucy heard some muffled words in the background, but they were indistinguishable due to the sobbing in her ear. After a moment, the sobs grew fainter and the voice got clearer. "Is this Lucy?"

"Yes. Who's this?"

"It's Jordan. Jordan Portman."

"What's wrong with your mom, Jordan?" Lucy reached for her boots. She had to be the last person on their list to call if they needed help with something. If she had to move, she wanted to be ready.

"Can you come to our house? And bring your tools?" Jordan asked.

"What's wrong?" Lucy repeated as she tugged on a shoelace.

"The bathroom faucets kind of exploded. My mom can't fix it and the super isn't home and my dad's out of town and the plumber costs too much and my mom's credit cards are maxed out," the teenager said in a rush. "We can't stop the water and if it hits the hall carpet, we'll lose the damage deposit."

She pulled on her other boot. "Listen to me, Jordan. I want you to look under the sink. You should see two pipes coming out of the wall. There should a hose leading up to the sink from each one. At the junction, there might be two little tabs that twist. If they're there, I want you to twist them. That should shut off the water."

While she waited, she did a quick check of her tool kit to make sure all her plumbing stuff was there.

"I turned them. The water stopped gushing."

"Good stuff, Jordan. Text me your address and I'll be over to see if I can fix whatever broke."

Her phone beeped in seconds with an incoming text.

"I'll be right there, Jordan. Mop up what you can with towels and throw them in the tub when you're done."

The teen's sigh was tremendous. "Thanks, Lucy."

"No problem."

She stopped in the maintenance room on the way out where there were half a dozen used faucet sets in there gathering dust. She picked a couple different sizes, threw them in a box, and added them to the pile of gear she was loading in her rental.

She hadn't been down this street in Holiday Beach. It was far from Main Street, and on the opposite side of town from the inn. Three small apartment buildings lined the block, and they all shared a connected parking lot. Lucy tucked the box of faucets under her arm and hefted her tool kit from the back seat. Jordan opened the front door for her.

"Thanks so much for coming over. Mom didn't

want me to call you at first, but I think she's okay now." She reached for the box. Lucy let her take it.

Brooke waited at the apartment door, pacing down the hallway. "Hi, Lucy," she said quietly.

"Hi, Brooke. I heard you sprung a leak."

"You could say that. Come on in."

They'd obviously tried to clean it up before she got there. She spotted a laundry basket full of soap and shampoo bottles and toothbrush holders on the kitchen table. It left her a clear workspace, but the bathroom was a mess. Water dripped from every surface, including the ceiling. Two halves of a hot water tap lay on the toilet seat.

"Yeah," Lucy said slowly. "This was probably horrifying."

"The tap just fell apart in my hand. It wouldn't stop spraying," Brooke said. "We managed to stop the water but now we have no bathroom sink."

Lucy set her toolbox on the edge of the bathroom. "Let's see if we can fix it."

The destruction was bad, but the damage to the plumbing was actually minimal. Once she verified the water was off, it took less than an hour to swap out the old taps and faucet. They didn't match the shower taps, but they worked. "Your super can replace those at his leisure, but they're good taps."

"Did you stop at the hardware store on your way over? How much do I owe you?"

Lucy shook her head. "These are old ones from the hotel. They were due to be thrown out, so don't worry about paying for them. I already recorded them as being destroyed."

"Thanks."

"I'm glad the Dew Drop Inn could at least do this for you." She made sure she could see Jordan watching television in the living room before she continued. "I really am sorry about Mr. Longfellow's news. I truly didn't know. When I got to Holiday Beach, I thought I was giving the hotel a new lease on life. I didn't realize I was keeping it on life support for a month."

Brooke teared up again. "I know. It just came as such a shock. It was a good job, and there aren't a lot of those around here. I don't know what I'm going to do. I was saving to go back to school, to get into some kind of program so I could be on more solid footing when it's time for Jordan to go to college. And now..."

"I'd be happy to write you a reference letter. I've got the connections to get you an interview with any Longfellow Family Hotel you want, but there aren't any around here. Minneapolis is the closest and that's too far for a commute."

"I couldn't move Jordan. I just have to have faith something will come up."

"Have faith and ask for help," Lucy said. "I'm in Holiday Beach for a few more days. Think about what you need and then talk to me, okay?"

"I will."

Lucy gestured at the bathroom. "Do you want help cleaning this up?"

"No, thanks. That's what a have a teenager for." Brooke offered her a small smile. "But I will ask if you can take all my towels and toss the in the hotel's washing machine. My laundry day isn't till Tuesday. I'll get them tomorrow."

"That I can do."

The bag of wet towels weighed twice as much as the box of taps and faucets, but Lucy eventually got them to the hotel's laundry room. She stayed up for an extra hour to make certain they got into the dryer.

She fell into bed with the realization she only had days left in Holiday Beach. She wasn't surprised so much had gone wrong on this assignment; that wasn't new. But the personal fallout was surprising. At least when she left, she'd be leaving one friend behind.

Lucy didn't know if Roy's angry parting words made things easier or harder to walk away, but either way she'd regret ending things the way they were. She'd honestly thought she and Roy had a chance.

With her luck, she should have known better.

CHAPTER 29

"ENTER." Roy glared at the computer screen and clicked his mouse again. "I said "Enter." Why aren't you entering?" he yelled at his computer. He should be at home enjoying a relaxing Sunday morning. He wasn't. He was in his office arguing with the new payroll program. Mickey had filled it in the previous week, and everyone was paid correctly.

Roy was preparing the next payroll period. So far, Emily was earning a hundred dollars an hour and he was paying eighty percent in state taxes. The help desk Mickey had bragged about still hadn't called him back. "Enter. Delete. Back-up. Give me a break," he begged.

When his pleading didn't work, he pulled out the big guns. "Mickey! Where are you?"

His brother appeared quickly, still holding a keg tap. "What's wrong? Why are you yelling?"

Roy gestured at the laptop. "It hates me. As assistant manager, you're getting additional responsibilities. Congratulations, you are now in charge of payroll." He gave Mickey what he hoped was a friendly smile. "Please make me get paid. I have no idea what I've done here."

"I'll think about it." But his brother grinned back.

Since he was on a roll, Roy continued. "I also owe you an apology about the order you put in. I checked my records. You were right. We did run short last year. I'm sorry."

Mickey's shoulders dropped a fraction, revealing a tension Roy hadn't noticed before. "Thanks."

"I know I have to stop thinking of you as a kid. You're much more than that. Give me some time to work on it, will you?" It would be a big change, but he'd better get used to thinking of Mickey as a partner instead of a responsibility. "If you have any other ideas, like this software or order tracking, let me know. I'll try to keep an open mind."

"And if you don't?"

"An ice cube down the back of my shirt will get my attention. You used to be good at that."

His brother laughed at the memory. "Mom helped." Mickey and his mom used to wake his teenaged-self when she handed little Mickey ice cubes to slip under the collar of the T-shirts Roy wore to bed. "But I will."

When the office phone rang, Roy answered it without looking at the call display. He'd been waiting for the program's help desk to call him back for over an hour. "Hello?"

There was a momentary pause before he heard, "Mr. Wagner, this is Lucy Callahan from the Dew

Drop Inn." Like he didn't recognize her voice. Then she continued. "As local next of kin, the hotel is calling to advise you that Harlan Longfellow is being taken by ambulance to the hospital in Bixby. He has authorized us to tell you that he was found weak but conscious in his room." She rattled off the phone number to the hospital's emergency room. "Thank you for your time."

And then she hung up on him. Before he could say a word.

"Who was that? Wrong number?" Mickey asked.

"Lucy."

"Really? What did she want?"

"To let us know that Harlan's being taken to the hospital."

For all he said he wanted nothing to do with his grandfather, the news was a blow. There was a difference between actively saying he hated the man and wishing him dead. Harlan was his mother's father. Although he hadn't grown up with the old man in his life, he had grown up with stories about him. They weren't all bad.

"Why did she call us?"

"She said something about local next of kin."

"What do we do?"

Roy had no answers.

"I think we should go," Mickey said.

"What? Why?"

"Because whatever he did to Mom, he's still our grandfather. What if he meant it when he said he came here to apologize before it was too late? Do you want to live with that guilt? Can you imagine what Mom would say if we did that?"

He didn't want to. But again, his little brother was right. Roy wasn't certain if he was in a place where he could accept Harlan's apology, but his mother would be ashamed of him if he didn't give the old man a chance to offer it.

"Let's put a sign up saying there was a family emergency in case we aren't back in time to open," he said.

"Do you want me to call Emily?" Mickey asked.

"Not today. Let's keep this in the family."

Mickey took the lead when they arrived at Bixby General Hospital. Roy had been there before, but it had been Mickey who had driven their mother to her treatments while Roy worked. Mickey knew the nurse working at the desk, and they were quickly escorted to a curtained cubicle at the end of the row.

Harlan looked terrible. His bloodshot eyes were vivid against his ashen skin, and the nasal canula snaking across his face made him look even frailer, if that was possible. Harlan blinked twice when he saw them. "I have to admit, I'm surprised you came," he rasped.

In that moment, Roy flashed back to his mother laying in a similar bed in the palliative care ward, saying the same thing when he would sneak in after hours. The nursing staff would call him if she were having a sleepless night, and he'd come by after finishing his shift. "You never knew us, but how could you not have come when your own daughter was dying? I know she sent you at least one letter." The words exploded from his mouth.

"Because I am a stubborn, arrogant fool," Harlan said. "I can't make excuses anymore. I already lost any chance I had for a relationship with my daughter. I'm hoping I still have a chance with her boys."

It was hard for Roy to admit he was wrong. Apologizing to Mickey earlier had been necessary but agonizing, and that was to his own brother. He couldn't imagine how hard it would be to apologize to a virtual stranger. When Harlan chuckled, Roy thought the old man was going to take it back and tell them it was a joke.

"You look just like my brother. He had the same look when I apologized to him. Like he'd accidentally swallowed a fly and couldn't believe it happened. He died before your mother was born. They were more alike than she and I ever were. I wish he'd been alive to meet her. I wish a lot of things had gone differently."

"How are you doing?" Mickey asked. Roy was grateful for the distraction.

"I had a cardiac incident. Not an attack, but the old ticker is starting to skip a beat every now and then. They've stabilized me but want to make sure it holds before they release me."

"Is it very serious?"

"I'm old. Everything is serious at my age. But I'm still here, and you're here, so I'm hoping this scare has pushed all of us down the right road. Since I've obviously scared you into showing up, I'm using this moment to say what I have to say." Harlan took a breath, the oxygen tubes in his nostrils shifting a little at the effort. He steeled his face, the gray skin wrinkling at the effort. "Your mother, my daughter, was always a headstrong girl. I thought it would do her well in business. I had plans for her to run the Dew Drop Inn while I built the next hotel. Then your father and his family entered the picture."

"Old man..." Roy didn't raise his voice, but his tone said it all.

"Your father was a good man. He just wasn't the man I wanted her to marry. I was so dead set on my plan for the family, I forgot she was family. It took me a long time to understand that. Pretty much until you were born," he said to Roy. "She sent me a birth announcement."

"What did you do?"

"Nothing. I'd let it snowball so much that by then I couldn't see a way back that managed to let me keep my pride intact. I never thought of a better way, and all of a sudden it was twenty years later, and she was dead and all I had left of her was a hotel I never got to give her. I dropped the Dew Drop Inn file in the bottom of a drawer and tried to forget it existed."

Now he had another thing in common with his grandfather: a tendency for avoidance. "How'd that work for you?" Roy asked.

"About as well as everything else I'd done with it up to that point. Then, instead of your mom, the hotel paid the price. That's why I arranged for the company's best property maintenance manager to visit. I had no idea it had fallen into such disrepair."

"Lucy's been working hard on it, hasn't she, Roy?" Mickey said.

Roy nodded slowly, appreciating his brother's loyalty to his new friend. "She's very good. She had local ordinances to deal with, complaints from neighbors, storm damage. You should have seen the hotel before she got here. The improvements she's made to the Dew Drop Inn over the past month are impressive."

"You sound like you like the old place."

"Mom talked about it a lot. More with Mickey than me, but she had plans."

Mickey snickered. "She used to call it the cubic zirconia in her imaginary crown. But, yes, in the abstract, the Dew Drop Inn has gigantic potential."

"How would you like to help it realize that potential?" Harlan asked. "I'm eighty-five years old, and I'm tired. If you're not interested, I'll sell the property. But I want to ask one more time if you want to keep it in the family. I'd like to be around to see what you do with it. Find out if you had the same plans for it as your mother did."

Mickey grabbed his arm, as if to stop him from turning Harlan down flat like he did the first time. Roy took a breath. Was it his place to tell Mickey he couldn't start a relationship with his grandfather? His baby brother wasn't a baby anymore; he'd proved that. Could Roy really hold him back when he was being presented with the opportunity of a lifetime?

"Will you take a gift from your stubborn old grandfather? It would mean the world to me to see the bar and the hotel working together like they were always meant to be." Harlan slumped against his pillow. The exchanged had been intense and seemed to have sucked up all of his energy. All he had the strength to do now was wait to see what they said.

"I have the bar. I want to keep it," Roy said. But he hurried to continue, "However, I wouldn't mind working with the Dew Drop Inn rather than fighting with it all the time." Old and sick or not, the old man wouldn't be comforted by lies. Roy had no desire to run a hotel. It had been his mother's dream, and his brother's apparently, but it wasn't for him. "Mickey?"

"I can't think of anything I want more than to turn the Dew Drop Inn into what Mom and I always knew it could be. But I don't want to leave you short, Roy."

"We'll make it work."

Harlan sighed and smiled. "I'll start the paperwork immediately. All I ask is that you keep me up to date. I assume you already have plans."

"Boxes of them."

"I'd be happy to look at them." Harlan jerked. "Not to critique. Just to see what you've come up with."

"I wish we could keep Lucy around. She'd make it all happen by the time tourist season starts," Mickey said.

Roy grimaced. "I'm pretty sure she's going to be happy to leave Holiday Beach."

"Why? I thought you two were getting along."

"I thought Harlan sent her to Holiday Beach."

"I did," his grandfather admitted.

"To spy on us," Roy continued. "I let her know I didn't appreciate the deception."

His little brother facepalmed at his admission. "I though you liked her."

"I did. It was why I got so mad." Now he owed somebody else an apology. But he wasn't sure if she'd accept one from him. He'd crossed the line.

"I'd never met Lucy Callahan before I got here. I picked her because of her reputation. Then I saw what she could do. She's worth every penny. I thought she was very impressive," Harlan said.

So did Roy. It would take some smooth talking to get her to a place where he could apologize. Even if she wasn't staying in Holiday Beach, she should know that he would welcome her back. And he'd make sure the rest of the town knew that she was part of the reason the inn wasn't closing. It was the very least he could do after he'd painted her in such a bad light.

Roy listened quietly as Mickey spoke to Harlan. He smiled at his brother's excitement. He and Mickey needed to have a long talk about the future. He didn't mind losing an assistant manager, but he wished he'd realized his little brother's dreams sooner. Of course, this was as good as the dream could get, so it turned out great. For Mickey. He was in so much trouble with Lucy, he couldn't see even a flicker of light at the end of the tunnel. If it hadn't been for Harlan, she wouldn't have spoken to him at all, and he couldn't blame her.

Harlan leaned back into his pillows with a little more color than he had when they arrived. "What are you going to do?"

"You could start with sending her flowers to thank

her for letting us know our grandfather was in the hospital," Mickey suggested.

His head throbbed as he tried to come up with an appropriate apology. "I think I need to do more than that."

CHAPTER 30

SMALL POTS of shamrocks with tiny gold foil leprechaun hats on sticks decorated the registration desk. A tiny black cauldron overflowing with gold coins sat on the coffee table in the lobby. And Lucy had never felt unluckier in her life.

Her time in Holiday Beach was coming to an end. For a trip that began on such a high note, it had been a long, hard fall. Her plan at the moment was to finish her work on the Dew Drop Inn, and then leave a dust trail behind her on the way out of town. For once she wouldn't mind moving on. She'd go home and look for a new place to set down roots.

Of course, it couldn't be that easy.

"You've got to be kidding me!" She hadn't meant to say it aloud, or that loud.

"What's wrong?"

At least Gloria was still talking to her. Lucy had helped her access a couple websites for her job search and had pointed her toward a handful of positions that weren't being advertised. It had helped smooth the waters and convince Gloria that Lucy hadn't come to the Dew Drop Inn with ulterior motives.

Lucy lifted her phone. "I just got notification from my landlord back in Boston. They've sold the building. I have a little third floor walk-up in a converted house. The new owners will not be renewing my lease. I have to be out by the end of May." There went her two-week staycation. She'd be packing and looking for a new place. At least she had a reason to insist that she work locally for the next couple months.

"If I end up in Boston, we could be roomies. I'd water your plants for you," Gloria offered.

Lucy laughed at the fact Gloria had remembered her stories of plant neglect. "If you end up in Boston, we'll talk."

Brooke arrived early. Usually, she arrived right at eight o'clock, or a couple minutes late. Gloria never minded, since Brooke would make up the time. "I'm here, I'm here," the blonde called on her way through the door.

"We see you."

"I'm on time, in case Mr. Longfellow is watching."

Lucy turned to Gloria. "Didn't you tell her?"

"I though you did."

Brooke gulped. "Tell me what. Please say it's not bad news and that our termination period starts early. I need the extra time to find..."

"That's not it," Lucy interrupted. "Everything is still on the same track it was last week. Mr. Longfellow was taken to the hospital yesterday. He stayed overnight. We don't know when he'll be back."

It had been scary finding him like that. When he hadn't shown up for their eight o'clock meeting by five minutes after the hour—which was twenty minutes late, according to his standards—Lucy had gone looking for him. After knocking on his door, she'd let herself in and found him lying on the floor, pale, sweaty, and gasping for air. The ambulance seemed to take forever. She hadn't realized it had to come all the way from Bixby. Harlan was doing better by the time it arrived, but thankfully he wasn't so stubborn as to refuse to go with them.

"That's horrible. Is he okay?"

"I think so. We haven't really heard anything."

"I wonder if he saw my super there," Brooke commented.

"What?"

"Our superintendent is also in the hospital. It's why nobody answered our emergency call on Saturday night," she explained. She sat on the sofa in the lobby and undid her winter boots, then pulled her uniform sneakers out of her shoulder bag. "Mr. Griffith is a sweet old man, but he should have retired years ago. The apartment block owners didn't want to push him out of his job. This may have forced their hand."

"If you have any more problems while I'm in town, give me a call," Lucy offered.

"You shouldn't be so nice to me after I blamed you for losing my job." Tears welled in Brooke's eyes for a moment, but she got her emotions under control. "You've been nothing but kind to me."

"You're a nice person. You deserved it," Lucy said.

Gloria's phone rang, and it broke the sombre mood. "Okay, let's get to work. I have new lighting fixtures to install in the Emerald Suite's bathroom, so that'll be fun. Then I get to paint it, so I'll be moving into another room for a couple days. I'll let you know when I'm done with it, okay?"

"That sounds good."

The biggest problem with swapping out light fixtures in the bathroom was that she had to turn off the only lights in the windowless room to do it. Lucy set one electric lamp on the vanity and another in the tub. Her lips went numb as she held a small but powerful flashlight in her mouth, but she got the job done.

She was just finished cleaning up when there was a knock on her door. Brooke stood in the hall, a hopeful look on her face. "Are you ready for lunch?"

A glance at the clock on the bedside table showed it was after one. "Sure." She had a sandwich in her mini fridge she was planning to eat in her room, but she grabbed it, a bag of chips, and a drink and followed Brooke to the staff room.

"My landlords called," Brooke told her as she cracked open a can of cola. "They asked me to pass along their thanks for your help. Flooding two apartments is a nightmare they were grateful to avoid."

"Tell them they're welcome."

"Then they asked if you were looking for work."

Lucy choked on her potato chip. "Excuse me?"

"I told them you were a property maintenance person, and they asked if you'd be interested in taking over for Mr. Griffith."

"Wow!" Lucy broke into a genuine smile for the first time in days. "That's flattering. They don't even know me."

"Maybe not, but they know me. And they know Julie Handler. I guess they talked to her about some of the repairs you did. Plus, the Mackenzie brothers were apparently talking about you around town, saying you knew your way around a paint roller."

"That was awfully nice of them."

"I know you mentioned that Holiday Beach is the type of place you'd like to settle down in. I thought you'd like to know that a lot of us would like to have you here."

Now it was Lucy's turn to have her eyes well up with tears. That was the nicest thing anyone had said to her in a long time. When she thought of finding a new apartment in Boston, the only thing she felt was inconvenience. She didn't know her neighbors. She didn't particularly care which neighborhood she ended up in. She wouldn't be there long enough to care. But this? Holiday Beach could have been everything she wanted. But after Harlan's announcement she assumed it would never be an option.

"Please tell them thank you for me. I wish I could talk to them about it."

"I will. If you change your mind, let me know. I wouldn't mind having you as a neighbor."

"Likewise."

Cementing the fact there were no longer any hard feelings, Brooke helped move Lucy's stuff to another room, then worked with her to move all the furniture in the suite away from the walls so Lucy could paint unencumbered. The pale gray paint she selected brought out the jewel-toned accents in the room. She didn't finish until late in the evening, but the overall look was worth it.

When she went downstairs to happily report to Gloria that the third suite was a day away from availability, she had to wait. A man with a box but no luggage stood at the desk, speaking intently to Gloria. The other woman nodded and accepted the package with a smile.

After he was gone, Lucy stepped up. "What's in the box?" she asked with a grin.

"I don't know. Why don't you open it? It is for you, after all."

Lucy was used to getting packages, but she had nothing coming in today. "Are you sure."

Gloria waved a card. Her brown eyes danced as she said, "Definitely."

Plumbing supplies didn't come with gift cards. "Give me that!"

She set the card aside and pulled on the flaps of the box. Nestled inside, with its pot carefully packed with balled-up newspaper, was her own small shamrock plant. Her heart jumped. She'd told Roy how cute she thought the plants were. Thinking it was an apology she reached for the card.

Gloria must have seen her smile falter. "Who's it from? Roy?"

"Yes."

"So why aren't you more excited?"

Lucy handed over the card. "To Lucy Callahan. From Roy Wagner" was all it said. No "I'm sorry for being a jerk." No message at all, in fact. She wondered why he'd bothered to send it in the first place.

"Well, he's trying."

"He'll have to do better than that." She deserved it.

CHAPTER 31

IT HAD BEEN TWO DAYS, and not a word from Lucy. Not even after he sent her the shamrocks. The message he'd put in the online order form was supposed to be the prelude to his big apology, but she hadn't acknowledged it, or him, at all.

On the other hand, saying it with flowers was a bit of a cop out, but it was the best he could manage. An hour after they'd left Harlan in the hospital, the doctors had called them back again after the old man suffered another "episode." It had taken into the evening before he was out of the woods, and after that, it was all Roy could do to stay awake until he made it home and fell into bed.

The next morning, the old man had called him at the crack of dawn to discuss transferring the property, and Roy got a crash course in real estate law that he'd never asked for. Lucy would have been thrilled—both about the inn and about him and Harlan being on speaking terms—but that wasn't something he could discuss with her till he'd apologized, and he couldn't take a break to make his apology until the paperwork was done and Harlan was doing better. It was a vicious circle that kept him away from her, and despite all he was gaining, he resented his family's windfall more by the minute.

Roy stretched his fingers, curled the tips like claws and stretched again. "My hand is cramping."

"Stop whining," Mickey retorted without looking up from the stack of papers in front of him. "Pretend you're famous and get back to signing and initialling."

Forty pages later and it was still Tuesday. St. Patrick's Day. William R. Truman the Third, Attorney-at-Law, had flown in the day before with a briefcase full of documents to start the transfer of the Dew Drop Inn over to its new owners. Roy had expected the bloated letter writer to be some stodgy, old, three-piece-suit wearing cross between Lurch and some old gray-haired English banker-type.

He'd had been right about the suit. The rest of his assumptions were blown out of the water when a six-foot-six tall Black man who was younger than him walked into the room. Bill, he learned, was the second generation of Truman lawyers to work for Harlan. He was slightly less officious in person than in his letters, but he still tolerated no nonsense when it came to paperwork.

They decided to set it up the same way as the bar, where he and Mickey would be equal owners, but while Roy managed the bar Mickey would run the hotel. His baby brother was ecstatic that he'd agreed to the deal. Mickey had only stopped talking long enough to grab a couple hours sleep before he showed up at Roy's door with By the Cup coffees and more plans to discuss.

Although he wished the old man well, Roy hadn't returned to the hospital to see his grandfather on Monday. He wasn't that ready to forgive yet. Mickey had gone and returned full of advice from one of the biggest hoteliers in the game, including a recommendation to keep on the existing staff for at least six months to help in the takeover. Harlan said he might want to reassess after that.

Roy had seconded the thought. "We should go over to the Dew Drop Inn and let them know what's going on. Brooke contacted me for a job, and I know that we're her last resort."

Mickey agreed. As soon as they were done with Bill, they were headed across the parking lot to start the Dew Drop Inn on a new chapter.

Bill returned the last file to his briefcase. "I'll send copies of these letters of interest to your lawyer. Then we can get into the real paperwork." He sounded excited about that.

"Yay, more signing."

"We'll send you a box of Longfellow Family Hotel pens," Bill promised.

"Gee, thanks," he replied a grin.

When it was time to cross the parking lot, Roy hesitated. As much as he wanted to talk to her, he was sure of what his reception was going to be after days of silence. And he deserved every bit of it. He could only hope that if he saw it through to the end, Lucy might be willing to forgive him.

"What's wrong?"

"Lucy's going to be there."

"She won't be much longer. She'll be heading home soon." Mickey gave his brother a hard look. "Is that a good thing or a bad thing?"

He tugged at his collar, trying to make it easier to choke out the word, "Bad."

"What are you going to do about it?"

"What can I do? 'Sorry I was a jerk' loses its effectiveness after the first time. Speaking of which, sorry I was a jerk. I should have noticed all the work you'd been putting in."

"I forgive you. I have to. You're family. But I appreciate it. I know that wasn't easy for you."

Roy laughed, and it sounded harsh to his ears. "I'm working on it. If I can get Lucy to accept my apology, maybe it'll help ease me down the path to being less of one in the future."

"I'm sure she'll understand about not seeing her sooner after you tell her about Harlan."

"What about before that?"

Mickey shrugged.

"I'm going to try, but if it doesn't work, she has no reason to stay in Holiday Beach. I won't have a second chance. It's not like the hotel can afford to keep her on full-time. She's very good at her job, which is why she can't stay forever."

"We still have to do all of the exterior. And the pool," Mickey suggested. A gust of damp spring air ruffled his hair. "She could work for us for a couple months while she looked for other work."

"That's a big ask. Hey, Lucy, would you like to quit your job in hopes that you find another one? I promise not to be a jerk again if you do."

"You don't get anything you don't ask for, Roy. No matter how much you want it. I think Harlan just proved that. His pride kept him from being happy with his family for more than twenty years. Don't let yours get in your way."

"How did my baby brother get so wise?"

"I got it from Mom."

"Smartass."

The bantering helped for a moment. Then they crossed the threshold of the Dew Drop Inn. Gloria Vargas was behind the registration desk on the phone, and Lucy was coming out of her office, screwing the lid on a thermos.

Gloria nodded in acknowledgment, leaving Lucy to speak to them. She didn't look thrilled at the opportunity. "Gentlemen. How can the Dew Drop Inn help you today? Is it about your grandfather? His room is exactly as he left it. Nobody's been in there."

"Harlan is recovering nicely after that first setback. Thank you for checking on him, and for calling the ambulance. When I saw him today, he thought the hospital would be releasing him tomorrow. He's going to rest here for a couple days, then fly back to Boston," Roy reported. Her cold, clinical tone rubbed him the wrong way, but at least she was speaking to him.

"I'm glad he's better." Then Lucy blinked. "Did

you say you went to see Mr. Longfellow in the hospital?"

He understood her confusion. "He came to see me after he saw you the first full day he was here. We had a discussion."

"A loud one," Mickey interjected."

"Then we had another one after you called, and we went to the hospital. And a couple more after that," Roy continued. He balled his hands into fists, and then forced himself to relax. He wanted to talk to her alone, but he needed everything else to be settled so he could finally give her his full attention like she deserved. "I'd like to talk to you about them but"—he gestured at Gloria, who was now off the phone—"we have other business first."

"Can we ask you to call Brooke down here, and whoever else is working today?" Mickey asked Gloria.

"It's just Brooke today. I'll find her," Gloria said.

Gloria left them in their little awkward bubble, and even Mickey felt the stress and wandered off, claiming he wanted to check out the tile work at the entrance.

Roy knew what he had to do. There simply wasn't a good starting point for that particular conversation. "The window looks good."

"It does."

"Sam mentioned he was getting a lot of attention from the pictures of the window you put online. In fact, a lot of people around town are grateful for what you've done at the Dew Drop Inn."

She met his eyes. "But not everybody."

"Some people are really slow when it comes to

recognizing a good thing, especially when it comes with change." He swallowed hard to get rid of the lump in his throat, because he really needed to finish. "But they can work on it."

He didn't have a chance to say more. Brooke followed Gloria back into the lobby. Both women stopped a few steps away and watched them suspiciously. "This is everybody," Gloria announced.

He nudged Mickey with his shoulder. Since his brother planned to take over the hotel, they decided he should be the one to make the announcement. "I know my grandfather, Harlan Longfellow, announced that he'd be selling the Dew Drop Inn. Those plans have changed. He's not selling the hotel, but it is transferring ownership. He's offered the property to me and Roy, and we've decided to accept the gift."

Gloria gasped. Brooke was more pragmatic. "What exactly does that mean?"

"It means the Dew Drop Inn is staying under the Longfellow Family Hotel Group, so nobody is getting fired."

Brooke crushed her hand against her mouth, trying to block her shocked cry. They all heard it anyway. "Are you sure?" The question ended with a sniffle.

"We're hoping you will all stay with us for at least the next few months. Changes may come later in the year, but for now, we're going on as we have been. We hope you want to stay with us and the Dew Drop Inn."

"I'm staying!" Brooke practically yelled her acceptance of the new arrangement.

"Good, because we need you," Roy said.

Gloria had let out a big sigh at the news but hadn't spoken. "Are you going to make any staffing changes? I like it here, but I've been waiting for them to fill the assistant manager position for over a month and I'm about to hit burnout."

Mickey stepped forward. "For now, you're looking at him." She didn't look relieved at the announcement. "I have a degree in hospitality management and experience working at a larger hotel. We can talk later."

Now it was Roy's turn. "We won't lie. This is going to be a big change for everybody involved. But we wanted everybody to know that their jobs were secure as we work through the process. Please keep coming to work, and we'll make sure you keep getting paid. Hopefully, before the summer season starts, we'll have new procedures in place. In the meantime, welcome to the new Dew Drop Inn."

Mickey asked Gloria if he could see which reservations system the hotel used and Brooke rushed off to text her daughter, leaving Roy and Lucy standing in the middle of the lobby. "I'm going to the parking lot to admire the attic window some more. Will you join me for a few minutes?" he asked.

"Let me get my coat."

"I'll wait!" He didn't mean to say it so loudly, but considering the alternative, the hopeful agreement burst from his lips. "Take as long as you need. I'll be here."

The surprise on her face hurt. He'd been so deep inside his own head before that he'd missed it, but if he'd caused this much pain, she must have had real feelings for him before everything went to hell.

He hoped he could get it back. He wasn't going to make another mistake with her.

They walked out together, Roy getting as close to Lucy as he could. He drew in long breaths of the fresh air. Spring was on the way. Snow on evergreen boughs melted and dripped onto sheets of ice that lay at the base of the trees. Birdsong was almost constant during the daylight hours, which were growing longer. In less than a month, winter would be a memory, and a month after that, Holiday Beach would be in full summer mode.

It wasn't right that Lucy was going to miss it.

"It does look good, doesn't it?" she asked. She didn't look at him. She kept her eyes fixed on the window.

"It looks great. Every change and repair you made to the Dew Drop Inn improved it. Even if other people thought they were unnecessary before you did them." That got her reluctant attention. "Harlan told us he questioned you on all your work. He also said that everything you did was justified. You made it much easier for Mickey to walk in and get to work. Now he doesn't need to worry the property itself, he just needs to learn the business."

She nodded at his compliment. "Mickey coming over to the hotel is going to leave you shorthanded at the bar, isn't it?"

"For a while," he admitted. "But when Emily is back from her trip to Los Angeles, I'll ask her if she's interested in stepping up. I think the Escape Room needs to evolve too. It's been stuck in the past for a while. There's a fine line between doing what's always worked and being stuck in a rut. I think I've been jolted out of it." He paused. "It was long overdue."

She twisted and looked him in the eyes. "That's a big thing to admit."

The tightness in his chest loosened. "It's not easy. I've had blinders on for a long time. That, and a whole bunch of pride. Which isn't a bad thing unless it's combined with blinders. I thought I had my fingers on the pulse of everything in this town. I never questioned it. Then you came to Holiday Beach. In the last month, you've touched so many people and places it's like you've been here for years. But because you're new, you saw it all with new eyes. You asked questions. You did what had to be done without worrying about excuses for why things had been left alone."

She barked out a laugh, but it wasn't a happy sound. "You make me sound like a hurricane."

He turned to face her head-on. He wanted her to see him, and he needed to see her. "I think you were more like a lucky tornado, one that picked up all the stagnant air and blew in new ideas and fresh starts."

"That doesn't sound like a good thing."

"It was for me. I didn't recognize it at first. I was too busy trying to hold on to handfuls of sand to realize there was gold in front of me."

He had Lucy's attention, but he could tell she was still wary by the way she held herself away from him. "Not everybody likes gold," she said.

He moved closer and released a slow breath when

she didn't pull back. "I think gold is beautiful. I think it makes everything better. I need more gold in my life."

"Roy..."

"I'm sorry, Lucy. I shouldn't have said what I did. It was wrong and it was untrue. Harlan's actions and consequences belong to him. Nobody else. Mickey had been trying to tell me he wanted more of a career than I was offering, and I refused to see it. That had nothing to do with you either. And as for how you fit in at Holiday Beach? You fit like you've always been here. I'm sorry I wasted a week of what little time we have left."

"Are you sure?"

He laid his hand on the side of her face. His fingers were cool, but her cheek was burning hot. He could hardly speak from fear of getting it wrong. "I'm positive that I'm sorry, and I'm absolutely certain that if I had a second chance with you, I'd make every second count. What do you say, Lucy?" Anything other than yes was unacceptable. He had plans for her. Easter, Memorial Day, Independence Day. The calendar was full of dates that he wanted to spend with her. Special ones and all the little ones, especially the little ones, in between. She held his future in her hands.

"I'm only here for a little while."

"I'll take it." He bent down, and when she gave him the barest nod, he kissed her like he'd wanted to do for days. It was everything he thought it would be. When he thought of all the times he'd missed out, he leaned in and kissed her again.

He needed a minute to catch his breath. "I'm really sorry," he said again, resting his forehead against hers.

"Thanks for apologizing."

"How long do we have?" Roy asked.

"About a week."

"Are you free tonight?"

"I'm free every night. It's in the Constitution," Lucy quipped.

"Very funny."

"I thought so."

Roy wrapped both arms around her waist and pulled her close. "I'm thinking Colombo's for dinner. Or the Atlas if I can't get reservations. But we're going to celebrate St. Patrick's Day tonight. Are you up for it?"

"You bet." She giggled. Then she full out snorted and burst into laughter.

"What's so funny?" Her giggles had him smiling and he didn't even know why. He had a feeling it would be happening a lot, and he looked forward to every time.

"This is the first time in my entire life when I ever had good luck on St. Patrick's Day. Holiday Beach must be my own personal good luck charm."

"Maybe you should consider sticking around then." He walked her back to the inn. "I know the Dew Drop still needs more work. Plus, you haven't seen the grounds. Or the pool You'll need at least a couple months to get them in order. I can ask Mickey to talk to your boss. He and the old man get along like a house afire." He hadn't had the same instant rapport with his grandfather that his brother did. But at least the possibility existed now for some kind of relationship in the future. "We could use somebody permanently. But not full-time," he admitted. "Please give us another chance."

She leaned back, studying him carefully. "Us? You, or Holiday Beach?"

"Both." But that wasn't what he wanted to say, and now wasn't the time to start playing shy. "Me. The town doesn't need you like I do. Please give me another chance."

Lucy surprised him. She wrapped her fingers around his and gave them a squeeze. Then she gave him a weird smile. "Remind me of this conversation again at supper. I have to make a phone call."

CHAPTER 32

THREE WEEKS LATER, Roy checked into the Longfellow Grand Bostonian Hotel after arriving on a late night flight. Harlan must have told the staff who he was, because Roy had never received so much attention in his life. He was in a suite, not the standard room he'd booked online. A fruit basket waited on the table that overlooked the Charles River. The bathroom was bigger than his bedroom back home. He stared suspiciously at the steam shower and wondered if he dare try it or if he would be accidentally steamed to death like a crab that wandered into a sauna.

He tapped his pocket again to make sure the package he'd brought from Minnesota hadn't gone missing. His luck had held for almost a month, but he wasn't going to start taking chances now. There was still a chance for things to go wrong, and he'd worked too hard to let that happen.

St. Patrick's Day had ended with the luckiest news he could have imagined. After his conversation with the staff at the Dew Drop Inn, and his private one with Lucy, Roy hadn't been certain of how the day was going to end. He managed to get a table at the Atlas by promising to update Habibah on everything that had transpired with Lucy.

"This afternoon, you asked me what it would take for me to stay in Holiday Beach," Lucy had said.

"That's right. I'd be happy to help you find a place. Like I said, we—the inn—needs more work that you're planning to do, but we don't have enough to keep you on permanently." He'd never thought that Lucy being so good at her job would be a problem. If she'd been less efficient, they'd have more left for her to do.

"What would you say if I told you had a full-time job offer here in town?"

"I'd say that was incredible news." Somebody was getting free drinks for life if they'd managed to talk Lucy into staying. "Where? Doing what?"

"The Franklins, Brooke's landlords, need a new superintendent for their rental complex. They offered me the job. It even comes with an apartment."

"That's lucky. Isn't it?" If it was perfect, wouldn't she have jumped on the opportunity already? His wine turned sour in his mouth as he considered the implications. Lucy would be going from an in-demand job at an internationally-renowned company to being a super in a town of less than ten thousand people. It wasn't a demotion, but it might feel like one. "It wouldn't be a good move for your career progression, would it?"

"Not if I wanted to move up with the company."

Roy reached for his wine glass, wishing it was

something stronger. That was a conversation ending comment.

Only it wasn't.

"On the other hand," she continued, "my managers have shown no sign of following up on my request for a permanent assignment in a city where I'd have enough work to stay there full time, and there are tons of places where that would be a possibility. You never want to be completely irreplaceable in your job, because that means you can never do anything else, and they consider me irreplaceable. If I want a change, I may have to take drastic measures. If the company won't work with me, I don't think I can work for them much longer."

He hadn't realized he'd been holding his breath. "That would be a big decision."

"Fortunately, I have a few days to figure it out."

Her smile had given him a little hope but no resolution to their dilemma.

At the end of the second week, Lucy had flown home. He hadn't known what her decision was. He threw himself into the bar, hiring a new bartender to replace Emily when she agreed to become the new assistant manager after her vacation, and helping Mickey bring Emily up to speed on her new responsibilities.

Then he got a call, inviting him to Boston to help her pack.

He'd booked the first available flight.

Now he was in Boston and the reality hit him. Here was a woman who was uprooting her whole life and starting a new job and he was one of the reasons. He already knew Lucy was adventurous; all her trips told him so. But this was jumping into a new situation with nothing more than confidence and luck. And her luck so far had been iffy at best.

He had to make sure she wouldn't regret it.

When Lucy picked him up the next morning, she had a large coffee and a four-pack of the biggest cinnamon buns he'd ever seen in a box on the passenger seat.

"Your car smells like heaven."

"I'll have to come back to Boston for these when the craving gets too bad," she said with a laugh.

"If they taste half as good as they smell, I'll drive." He'd happily drive to Timbuktu if she was beside him.

They spent the morning packing the rest of her bookshelves and taking photos and paintings off the wall. After they made room to sit on the sofa, Lucy told him her plans for her new place. "It's a two-bedroom unit, which sounds decadent after this place. But since I'll actually be living there instead of only visiting it a few days a month, I suppose I'll need the space. I'm going to turn the second bedroom into an office with a pull-out sofa for when I have guests over. After talking up Holiday Beach so much, I already have requests for the Fourth of July."

"You'll love Minnesota in the summer. You'll be outside every single day. Our public beach is amazing. Plus, you haven't experienced any of our food trucks yet. They're a culinary experience on their own. You've only seen a sliver of what we have to offer." If she thought the community was friendly in the dead of winter, she should see it when the weather was on their side. She'd never want to leave.

He called an early quitting time after spending four hours packing up her tiny kitchen. He had no idea how she'd wedged so many pots and pans into the half-dozen drawers and cupboards. "Note to self. Never challenge Lucy to Jenga," he joked.

"I will also beat the pants off you in any Lego challenge. Be warned." She pointed to a large rubber storage container whose lid was taped on tightly. "It's full of Lego blocks. Full," she emphasized.

A grown woman having a box of kids' toys sounded a bit weird. But he'd heard the same thing about fantasy football pools, so he wasn't about to judge. "Those will be good for snow days next winter," he said.

He'd arranged to take Lucy out for dinner on his second last night in Boston when he learned it would be her birthday. It had taken a lot of research, and a personal recommendation from William Truman the Third, but he'd scored reservations at *L'Oeuf de Caille*. After he looked it up online, he'd made a special trip to Bixby to have his best suit dry-cleaned. Then he'd called up a translation website and made his way through the French menu, so he knew what he was ordering.

When he told Lucy where they were going, she nodded in sudden understanding. "Now your insistence on not packing my shoes and dresses makes sense. I'll be dressed to the nines when you pick me up."

There was no way he was letting her drive to her

own birthday dinner. Fortunately, he had a grandfather with a car and driver who was trying to make up for lost time. Roy showered and shaved and took an extra minute with his tie to make sure it was perfectly straight. Then he tucked the slim velvet box he hadn't let out of his sight for the last week into his blazer pocket and headed to the lobby to start his night on the town. If everything went according to plan, it would be the start of a new chapter in his life. One he couldn't wait to write with Lucy.

Boston in springtime had a hum in the air that wasn't frantic, but still full of energy. People had shaken off the snow and were out enjoying the milder weather and longer days. The car dropped them off a couple doors down from the restaurant, which was as close as it could get because of construction.

Lucy wore a red dress he'd never seen before. Her hair was pulled up in a fancy twist, and although he didn't know exactly what she'd done, her makeup made her look more sophisticated than he'd ever seen her. He was used to Construction Lucy, but tonight she was showing off another facet, like the diamond she was. "You look beautiful."

"This place is very nice," Lucy said. "I've never been here, and I live in Boston. How did you find out about it?"

"Harlan's lawyer recommended it. I wanted to take you somewhere special for your birthday."

The plush chairs were spaced well apart, and flanked a heavy wooden table covered with a thick white linen cloth. Low classical music played in the background. The menu was less intimidating than it would have been if he hadn't done his research first. Usually, if Roy found a dish he liked, he ordered it every time. Lucy, on the other hand, had tried something new every time she'd gone to the Atlas or Colombo's. Tonight, he was going to follow her example, and he ordered the roasted quail, the roasted parsley potatoes, and a root vegetable medley. She ordered the Boeuf Bourguignon, which came with a basket of French bread rounds.

The meal was quiet but pleasant. They were both tired from a full day of packing boxes, and they knew they still had one day left. After that was a two-day drive back to Minnesota.

"Are you absolutely, positively certain you want to do this?" Roy asked. "I know I want you to, but it's going to be a big change."

"I've been thinking about this for a long time," Lucy admitted. "I didn't have a specific destination in mind, but I knew a change was on the horizon. I like property maintenance and I'm tired of living out of suitcases. This will give me the best of both worlds. Plus, there are some other benefits to moving to Holiday Beach." She lay her hand on the table and he quickly reached out to hold it.

He gave her fingers a gentle squeeze for luck. And courage. "I think it's auspicious that you're starting a new year in a new place, give or take a day. Speaking of which..." He drew the black velvet box from his pocket and slid it across the table. "Happy birthday."

"What is this?"

"A birthday present."

He reluctantly let her go. Her hand hovered over the box.

"Aren't you going to open it?" he pressed.

"My present was you coming to Boston. I didn't expect this."

"I did. Open it." He wanted to see her reaction.

"It's beautiful," Lucy exclaimed. "It's the perfect thing to mark my first visit to Holiday Beach and meeting you." She tilted the box, and the fine gold chain caught the light and shone brightly, but it was the small diamond in the gold shamrock pendant that really sparkled.

Roy stood and walked behind her to help put it on, stealing a kiss on her neck while he was at it. When he retook his seat, he couldn't help but say, "It looks great on you."

She gently touched the shamrock charm. "I love it."

"Maybe Santa will bring you another piece for Christmas." There was no "maybe" about it. He'd already bought the matching earrings. "I know it's been a little more than a month, which seems fast. But it's also you, so it's also seems like I've known you forever. I want there to be no doubt about my feelings for you. This is the first, but not the last, special occasion I intend to spend with you. I'm in love with you, Lucy."

"That works for me, because I love you too, Roy."

He stood again and walked around the table just to kiss her when she said that. He couldn't help it. From the sighs of the couple at the next table, and from

Lucy's welcoming response, it was definitely the right move.

Lucy was blushing when he sat back down. "I've told you how I'm never lucky when it comes to myself," Lucy said, "but I think you and Holiday Beach have finally broken that streak."

Roy hated to break it to her, but she was wrong. "I hope your luck has changed for your sake, but I can tell you it's definitely still affecting other people. Because you, Lucy Callahan, are my lucky charm."

EPILOGUE

THE LONGFELLOW FAMILY Hotel in Toledo, Ohio was the halfway point between Boston and Holiday Beach. After seven hundred miles of driving and junk food snacking, Lucy planned to spend the next hour in the shower trying to work out the kinks while Roy did the same in his en suite bathroom in their adjoining suites. Then they were supposed to meet for a light, healthy supper before heading to bed early to have an even earlier start the next morning to finish their journey to Lucy's new hometown.

But first she had to return the five messages Brooke had left on her phone. "What's going on? Is there a problem with the apartment?" Brooke had offered to clean it in anticipation of Lucy's arrival, and she was grateful to have that one task off her plate.

"The apartment is fine. Aaron Gillespie is the problem."

Lucy blinked at the phone. "Sheriff Gillespie? Are you in trouble? Is Jordan?"

"No, he just keeps stopping by the Dew Drop Inn and talking to me."

Lucy chuckled. "You mean he's flirting?"

"I think so. It's weird! I need some advice from somebody who's been around the dating block as an adult."

"Hey, I'm not a 2009 Toyota," Lucy protested.

"You know what I mean. What do I do?"

"Flirt back?"

"I can't." Then Brooke let out a deep sigh that almost had Lucy offering sympathy.

"Why not?"

There was another sigh, but no answer.

"Because he's cute?" Lucy prodded.

"Yes. And I'm out of practice. And even if I wanted to, I don't have time. I work. I have a teenager. And other commitments."

"Those are terrible excuses." But Lucy understood. Putting herself out there when it came to Roy was the hardest, bravest thing she'd ever done. But it had paid off for her.

"They're the only ones I have!"

"Well, you'd better come up with better ones by the time I get back to Holiday Beach, or I'm going to be on Aaron's side."

"Some friend you are."

Lucy laughed. "Good-bye, Brooke. I'll see you tomorrow."

She was still snickering when Roy knocked on her door to take her to the restaurant. He was back in his usual flannel shirt and jeans, his suit carefully stowed in his suitcase. "What's so funny?" he asked.

"Of all the virtues you raved about, you neglected to mention Holiday Beach was a hot-bed of romantic intrigue."

His befuddled expression was adorable. "What are you talking about?"

She linked her arm through his and walked him to the elevator. "This is going to be fun."

THE END

If you enjoyed this story, please sign up for Elle's newsletter to hear about new releases in the series at www.ellerush.com/newsletter.

ABOUT ELLE RUSH

Elle Rush is a sweet romance author from Winnipeg, Manitoba, Canada. When she's not travelling, she's hard at work writing books which are set all over the world. From Hollywood to the house next door, her heroes will make you swoon and her heroines will have you laughing out loud.

Elle has a degree in Spanish and French, barely passed German, and has flunked poetry in every language she ever studied, including English. She also has mild addictions to tea, yarn, her vegetable garden, and bad sci-fi movies.

MORE FROM ELLE RUSH

SWEET CONTEMPORARY ROMANCE

Hopewell Millionaires

Doctor Millionaire
Fall a Million Times
A Million Love Notes (coming Summer 2022)

Holiday Beach

Shamrocks and Surprises
Pumpkins and Promises (coming October 2021)

North Pole Unlimited

Decker and Joy
Hollis and Ivy
Nick and Eve
Rudy and Kris

Ben and Jilly
Frank and Ginger (coming Fall 2021)

Resort Romances

Cuban Moon
Mexican Sunsets
Dominican Stars
Mayan Midnights
Complete series 4-book box set

COOKBOOKS

Heartmade Collection

Brunch
Mains and Sides
Holiday Table

CONTEMPORARY ROMANCE

Hollywood to Olympus (also in paperback)

Screen Idol
Drama Queen
Leading Man
It Girl
Action Hero
Complete series 5-book boxed set

Made in the USA
Coppell, TX
19 October 2022

84993102R00154